"Come lie w~~ith me,~~
he murmured

As T.C. held out his arms, Tessa slipped
gratefully into them. His lips on hers were
hungry and urgent, and Tessa felt molten
desire moving up her body.

The stars shone above the trees, the
crackling fire warming them as their bodies
moved together. They breathed deeply of
the scents of the forest and the fragrance
of each other's bodies. Tessa's nipples
hardened as she shed her blouse. She
reached out to draw T.C. closer.

"Relax," he whispered, leaning down to kiss
her belly. "We have all night...."

THE AUTHOR

Jill Bloom has been a chef in a French restaurant, a dancer and a journalist. On a dare she wrote and sold her first novel. Then she learned how to type!

Jill now keeps busy as a Boston journalist and an enthusiastic writer of romance novels. She and her husband, a jazz musician, have one daughter and live "in an atmosphere of fond chaos."

Two of a Kind

JILL BLOOM

Harlequin Books

TORONTO • NEW YORK • LONDON
AMSTERDAM • PARIS • SYDNEY • HAMBURG
STOCKHOLM • ATHENS • TOKYO • MILAN

Published December 1984

ISBN 0-373-25137-8

Printed in Canada

1

THE AFTERNOON SHUTTLE FLIGHT from D.C. banked steeply over the city of Boston. Tessa Drew leaned forward in her seat and, after fighting back a brief wave of vertigo from the acute angle of her view, began to make out familiar landmarks. It was a beautiful sight—the winding grid of streets, the brick town houses interspersed with sheer high rises and the impudent curve of the Charles River cutting a silver swath through it all.

It would be warm when she landed—perhaps not as warm as Baltimore had been, but one of those sunny prescient days that herald the long-awaited arrival of spring. Such days, Tessa had always felt, were an extravagance of nature.

The plane ride had been an extravagance, too, but Tessa felt she deserved it. Douglas Bright, with whom she had had a steady relationship for the past three years, had just broken off with her, telling her that if she walked out of his life now she could never come back.

And she had. She had stood there for an awkward moment on the street in Baltimore, staring at Douglas's angry face as if it belonged to a complete stranger and wondering how she should handle this unexpected situation. But even as she wondered, she found herself turning slowly to walk away from him, moving out to the curb to hail a cab, feeling like an actor in a role she had not chosen to play. Still, she had not turned around, even though she could feel Douglas wanting her to with an almost palpable force. She did not even look back as she got into the cab and gave instructions to be taken to Dulles. She had walked right out of his life.

And she had been waiting ever since that moment for the reality of what she had done to hit her with pain, remorse, guilt—anything that would signal to her that she had made a drastic mistake, as she assumed she had. She had been waiting all morning, probing at her emotions as one would a sore tooth. But nothing had happened. There was a mild sensation of surprise and a vague feeling of aimlessness, as if she had lost her bearings in a familiar place. That was all.

The truth was, she had always considered her relationship with Douglas to be ideal. For the past three years they had seen each other almost every weekend, alternating between Baltimore and Boston, between his apartment and hers. There had been some discussion about the cost and inconvenience of the commute—Tessa could not afford to fly when it was her turn, as Douglas did—and about how nice it would be if they both got great jobs in the same city someday. But neither of them had ever considered giving up what they already had.

And then, out of the blue on this sunny spring morning had come his ultimatum. "Either you move down here and try to get a job in Baltimore or we break it off completely—now." Douglas had said he was tired of the commute and tired of being odd man out when the other anchormen got together during the week for dinner with their wives. "If you really loved me," he had said bitterly, "you'd move here to be with me without giving it a second thought."

Well, she had really loved him—or thought she had. They had met while covering the 1980 presidential primary in New Hampshire. Douglas was a political reporter for the network affiliate in Baltimore, and Tessa had just joined WBOS, Channel 8, in Boston as a feature reporter. She and Douglas had enjoyed each other's company, exchanging gossip about their co-workers over seafood in casual restaurants featuring fresh clams and oysters and wandering through crowded shopping malls eating ice cream and holding hands.

It had suited Tessa just fine. It also suited her that they spent time apart during the week when she could concentrate on her career at WBOS. She also needed time just to be by herself. Tessa felt committed, but not smothered. If anyone had asked her to respond instantly to the word "love," she probably would have said "Douglas."

But today Douglas had accused her of not being committed, of being irresponsible, of not caring about things that mattered. He was ready to settle down, he had said—this was the first she had heard of it!—and it was up to Tessa to agree to his terms. The future of their relationship, he had told her, was in her hands.

And she had walked away from it, without even really knowing why. All the way home she had been waiting for the horror of what she had done to hit her. She felt a familiar sense of inadequacy. Was she really that selfish? That detached from her emotional needs?

She had heard those questions before in her thirty-three years. She had sometimes wondered what it was that set her apart from her friends, that made her draw back from total involvement. It was as if a little imp were sitting on her shoulder, watching and enjoying the fun until the moment came to say, "Really, is this worth it? Does this really mean that much to you? Come on, be honest."

And the little imp was usually right. Half in jest, Tessa referred to the imp as her twin, reminding herself that she had been born under the sign of Gemini, the ever-mutable Twins. Was it any wonder she could never settle down and commit herself to anything?

But that wasn't true. She was committed—to her job, to her friends and, she had thought, to Douglas. And now, returning to her apartment in Boston on a Saturday afternoon with an unclaimed weekend stretching before her, she had to question that commitment, or lack of it. Blaming the ever-mutable Twins made fine cocktail chatter, but Tessa was beginning to wonder if there wasn't something wrong with her. Did being a Gemini mean she would never commit herself to anyone? That she would spend the rest of her life alone and emotionally detached, trying to analyze and reanalyze feelings that weren't even really there? The only feeling Tessa could summon on this sunny Saturday afternoon was a feeling of guilt because she felt so little.

Back in her South End apartment, even the guilt disappeared. Tessa felt a curious sense of laziness, as if she were living inside a stolen wrinkle of time. She felt content to sit in the window seat in her living room and watch the bird feeder she had placed outside her bay window on Friday, waiting for the birds. And waiting to feel something.

Then the phone rang. Tessa jumped. She was sure it was Douglas calling to apologize. Who else would know she was home on the second Saturday in the month?

But it wasn't Douglas. It was Lucinda Kane, her close friend. And she, of all people, should have known that Tessa was in Baltimore.

"What on earth are you calling me here for?" Tessa demanded.

"What on earth are you doing there would be the more important question, don't you think?" Lucinda replied. "Anyway, you know I'm a witch. I got the vibes that you were at home and in need of me."

"Don't be silly," Tessa replied. She was somewhat annoyed that her solitude had been interrupted. She had been rather enjoying sitting there with no plans and no commitments, nursing her nonwounds and waiting.

Lucinda sighed. "If only you had a more receptive attitude toward my supernatural powers," she said. "The world is not completely rational, you know. It's full of surprises."

"I know. I got a big surprise this morning," Tessa said.

"Ah, so I was right in my premonition. The Voice of Baltimore has been giving you a hard time, hasn't he?"

There was no love lost between Lucinda and Douglas, each of whom thought the other was superficial. Tessa had long ago stopped trying to mix the two of them socially when Douglas was in Boston.

"Please, Lucinda, spare me your I-told-you-so's. Let's just say the Voice got a little strident and leave it at that." In spite of herself, Tessa grinned. *I shouldn't be so flippant*, she reminded herself sternly.

"I promise, not a whisper of triumph," Lucinda replied solemnly. "However, I will take it upon myself to try and cheer you up. It's the least I can do for a heartbroken friend."

"I'm not sure I want to be cheered up." Tessa was already beginning to lose interest in the conversation. She was tired and, if not exactly heartbroken, at least a little bruised. The idea of spending the weekend hiding out in her apartment was growing more and more appealing.

"Oh, but you really should put in an appearance at this event," Lucinda told her. "After all, you're supposed to be one of the honored guests."

"Honored guests? What event?" Tessa frowned, then clapped her hand to her forehead and groaned. "Oh, Luce, this isn't that Boston Best Bash you're planning on dragging me to, is it?"

"Dragging you? My dear, you're the one who won a Boston Best award, aren't you? Didn't you know the party was tonight? Don't you ever read the news-papers?"

"Lucinda, I work in a newsroom, remember?"

"*I* remember. Don't *you* remember that you won an award for Best Investigative Reporter for a Human Interest Story? And that the Boston Best Society would appreciate your acting properly honored by showing up at their bash?"

"I forgot it was tonight. Not that I would have gone, anyway. I'm supposed to be in Baltimore, re-member?" Tessa began to feel a thickness in her throat. *Here it comes,* she thought resignedly. *I should be feeling properly miserable any moment now.*

Lucinda's voice was tart. "You should be doing what *you* want, not wearing a rut in the road from here to Baltimore like some insane hamster. Now, do you want to go or not?"

"I don't like parties."

"Wrong. Douglas doesn't like parties. You do, or you used to, before the Voice convinced you other-wise."

"Now wait a minute. Douglas never made me do anything I didn't want to do! I wouldn't be back here now if he had." As soon as she said it, Tessa knew it was true. She had rejected Douglas's ultimatum not because she felt she needed more time to think, as she had told him, but simply because she did not want to do it. She liked Douglas, probably even loved him. But she did not want to leave her job or Boston to move to Baltimore.

It all seemed simple when she looked at it that

way. And the lump that had been building in her throat disappeared at once. It was going to be nasty for a while, being without someone after feeling safe and secure for so long. But she had done the right thing.

"Tessa? Are you still there?" Lucinda's voice sounded uncertain for the first time.

"Yes, I'm here. And you're wrong about parties, Lucinda. I never really did like them. Especially not the kind where everybody runs around patting everybody else on the back, even if they don't know them. And especially not when I'm one of the ones who's supposed to get patted. I'm very particular about my back, you know, Lucinda."

"Yeah, yeah, yeah. I'll pick you up at eight."

And Lucinda was gone before Tessa could tell her she would go—just this once.

ACTUALLY, by the time eight o'clock came around, Tessa was in no mood to go anywhere at all. As she had expected, the situation with Douglas had come up and hit her from behind. She was feeling quite bereft, and several times during that long afternoon Tessa even considered calling him up and telling him she had changed her mind. After all, she probably could get a job in Baltimore, and Douglas was perfectly normal to want a commitment from her after so many years, and what was wrong with her, anyway, that she could walk away so easily from three wonderful years?

It also hurt her that he had let her leave. Why hadn't he tried another tack when he realized the tough stance wouldn't work on her? What was he feeling right now, alone in Baltimore on a Saturday for the first time in three years? He shouldn't have let her go.

The lump in her throat had returned to stay, and when Lucinda pounded on her door, Tessa was only half-dressed. She would tell Lucinda she couldn't make it.

"Are you sick?" Lucinda's thick brows knit together in concern when she saw her.

"Not sick." Tessa sniffled. "Just miserable."

"You are?" Lucinda seemed truly surprised to hear it.

"Of course I am!" Tessa snapped. "Why shouldn't I be? The man I've been with for three years suddenly kicks me out because I won't move in with him, I'm all alone, I probably made the worst mistake of my life, and now you want me to grin and bear it at this ridiculous hugfest for local semicelebrities? How do you think I feel?"

Lucinda pursed her lips. "Sounds like you feel exactly the way you're supposed to feel," she observed. Then, catching Tessa's narrowing glare, she went on, "Which is exactly why I am taking it upon myself to drag you out to this little hugfest, as you so charmingly put it." She took Tessa by the shoulders and began corralling her into the bathroom. "A classic case of heartbreak like yours needs a classic diversion, and there's nothing more diverting than a Boston Best Bash—especially when you're one of Boston's Best."

THE FACT THAT TESSA was going to the Boston Best Bash at all was unusual. And when she learned that the festivities were not in one of Boston's gilded hotel ballrooms but on a large and distinctly rocky cruise boat scheduled to make a few quick circuits around the windy inner harbor, Tessa realized that the day's events were moving from the unusual to the improbable. Who could possibly have imagined that level-headed, rational Tessa Drew, Best Investigative Reporter for a Human Interest Story (according to the Boston Best Society), would find herself on the first night after her breakup climbing the gangplank of a large, crowded and rocky boat? *Now*, Tessa thought bleakly, *I'll feel guilty, lonely* and *seasick.*

At the precise moment she stepped off the gangplank onto the deck of the boat, she saw something that escalated the improbable into the impossible. Tessa felt the floor pitch suddenly beneath her and grabbed Lucinda's arm to right herself. She wasn't sure if it was the boat or her own sudden loss of equilibrium.

It was like looking into a mirror—a slightly distorted mirror, to be sure, but not one that made the image grotesque. No, the man she saw a few feet away was quite clearly handsome. He was dark, slender and of medium height. His brown-black hair arched away from a high forehead in a smooth swath of color. His cheekbones reflected the fluorescent light without appearing shiny—"velvety" was how she would describe the tone of his skin. His mouth was wide and his lips full, and the chin beneath it was strong but well-rounded. His body was firm but compact, as if he engaged in a solitary sport like running rather than a group sport like tennis or racquetball.

But it was his eyes that caught and held her, just as

she knew hers had captured his attention. The man's eyes were wide spaced but deeply set at a slight angle, just as hers were. They were tawny brown and, even from a distance, she saw the highlights of gold and green. Just like hers.

It was not a mirror image, more like déjà vu—as if Tessa were seeing herself as she might have been, given the slightest genetic wrinkle. The fact that he seemed to be of Eurasian ancestry and she was half Irish, half Italian seemed to make perfect sense. Of *course* they could look alike! The fact that her hair was lighter than his, that her nose went on into long, delicate nostrils while his began to turn up at the very tip—all of this made perfect sense.

He saw it too, she could tell. He had been standing with a small knot of people along the windows that looked out onto the water. He turned, saw Tessa and froze in quarter profile, so that the blue of the water created a strong, back-lit effect. He could have been cast in a portrait. And his eyes, when they registered Tessa, widened and darkened, just as she knew hers had done. He opened his mouth slightly as if about to speak, and she saw small, white teeth. She resisted the impulse to part her lips in exactly the same manner.

Lucinda was transfixed, too. She had stopped, looked back to see why Tessa had paused, followed Tessa's gaze and clapped a hand to her mouth.

"Holy cow!" She grabbed Tessa's arm. "Do you see that?"

"Of course I do." Tessa saw the man's eyes register Lucinda's reaction, but his expression did not alter. He was not smiling or showing any shock, although Tessa knew he must have felt some. He seemed to be simply absorbing the sight of her. She tried not to react to Lucinda's tugging, and she didn't take her eyes off the man.

"For God's sake, that's the weirdest thing I ever saw!" Lucinda whistled softly between her teeth. "Do you know who that man is? I've got to find out who he is. I wonder who knows him. . . ."

Lucinda took off through the crowd, and Tessa followed. It was from that moment on, as she later surmised, that events slipped from her control and into the realm of the extraordinary.

Tessa allowed Lucinda to drag her on a whirlwind tour of the upper and lower decks, accepted and drank the glass of wine she was handed, but refused a second. She responded with the proper degree of enthusiasm and modesty to the congratulations she received from well-wishers, and she promised the chairperson of the Boston Best Society that in future she would RSVP as requested. She also agreed to stand up and take a bow when her name was called during the awards speeches. Tessa then congratulated the other Boston Best award winners she met with just the right combination of appreciation and irony, and she allowed herself to be patted on the back a number of times.

But mostly, she was just waiting. Waiting for Lucinda to do what she did so well—finagle an introduction to a total stranger.

It didn't take long. Only minutes went by while the boat moved noisily alongside the dock, and the party on board got increasingly raucous. There was something about being detached from solid land, even at the dock, that made time irrelevant. But for Tessa, the moments were endless.

Finally, Lucinda met up with an ex-lover who was a casual acquaintance of the stranger, and he offered to introduce them. When they came up to the man he turned and seemed not at all surprised to find himself face-to-face with Tessa. She stood quietly, looking at her strange mirror image.

His name, she heard, was Thomas Chimatsu, but everybody called him T.C. He was an environmental engineer with a prestigious firm in Cambridge, and his specialty was aquatic and harbor engineering. As a matter of fact, he had been awarded a Boston Best award for a wildlife sanctuary he had built on re-claimed land from a huge estate on Cape Cod.

"I remember hearing about it," Tessa murmured. She had been expecting the man to shake her hand or at least to smile, to indicate his reaction to a pretty woman. She even looked down expectantly at his hands, which were wide and square and neatly groomed. But he remained very still throughout the introduction. His expression remained pleasant, but not aggressively so.

She did remember the Elliott Sanctuary. There had been some hue and cry because, in order to build the preserve, acres of natural swampland had had to be dredged. Some environmentalists had scoffed that it was like filling in a lake to build a swimming pool, although others had pointed out that the swampland was eroding badly anyway.

"I suppose congratulations are in order for you,

too, then," she added after a rather long pause. So far, T.C. had not congratulated her—he hadn't said a word. She wanted to hear his voice. "Congratulations," she finished lamely. She wished Lucinda would stop staring at them.

"On the Elliott Sanctuary or on the Boston Best award?" His voice was deep and pitched low, so that he seemed to be sharing a secret with her alone, although they stood in a group. The voice was strong for that compact frame, and surprisingly warm.

"On both, I guess," she replied.

"I'm proud of the Elliott Sanctuary," he said, smiling a private sort of smile.

Tessa felt relief loosen her smile into a grin. She sensed that he shared her ambivalence about the Boston Best Bash, and the award. Ever since she had been notified of the honor by the Boston Best Society, a group of local critics and chamber-of-commerce types who took their annual mission very seriously, she had been unsure of how to react. She had been given her award for a four-part series titled, "Why Kids Split—The Story of Three Runaways." And while she appreciated the recognition and understood its value in terms of her career at Channel 8, she had always secretly felt that the story had not been her best. She had allowed herself to get too maudlin in her reporting. Not because she felt it—for she had taken care to avoid personal involvement with her three teenaged subjects—but because she had known it would sound good on the air.

T.C. seemed to have no such ambivalence about his achievement and no undue pride, either. He mere-

ly accepted it as fact. She liked that. And she liked
the fact that while he seemed perfectly at ease in this
crowd, there was a part of him that was clearly not
present, just as a part of her was not.

"You must be proud of your reporting work for the
Focus Team," T.C. said after a pause, as if he was
waiting for her to finish her thoughts. "I've enjoyed
your work, when I have the chance to see it." He
spoke as if Tessa's skills, too, were a matter of fact,
not taste.

"Did you catch Tessa's series on teenaged runaways? That's what got her the Boston Best." This
came from Lucinda, who was obviously getting into
the role of facilitator.

T.C. gave her a glance that was both appreciative
and dismissive. "I'm afraid not," he said politely, and
turned immediately back to Tessa.

The conversation suffered another awkward
pause, although T.C. did not appear to feel ill at
ease. He searched Tessa's face patiently, as if he were
looking at himself in a mirror. But he made no comment on their resemblance. His gaze simply moved
across her features in a leisurely fashion that with
any other man she would have found offensive.

But Tessa could not help doing the same thing. In
her two-inch alligator heels she was almost as tall as
he was. The close resemblance as she looked directly
into his eyes was almost dizzying. She wondered if
the boat had started to pitch more heavily. T.C.
seemed to be standing perfectly still, silently offering
her the opportunity to catalog his features, as he was
cataloging hers.

Up close he seemed less small boned and more powerful than he had at a distance. She could sense the disciplined lines of his torso beneath the neat, slightly preppy tan jacket. Maybe not a runner, she decided—maybe a swimmer, or perhaps a wrestler. No, he looked too controlled to engage in a violent contact sport. Powerful, but controlled.

Tessa herself had done a fair amount of swimming as a girl, and she had been a good gymnast, too, with her slightly broad shoulders, small breasts, slim hips and powerful haunches. But she had never been committed enough to one sport or the other to get serious, and even now her attempts to recapture that feeling of power and flexibility were sporadic, to say the least.

She was fascinated by the differences between them as well as their similarities. His eyes were a bit darker than hers, and they angled up at a more definite tilt than hers did, though they were too deep-set to have a classically Oriental shape. His brows were thicker than hers and, where hers embraced the top of her lid in a wide curve, his ended in a feathery lift that gave him a slightly quizzical expression. His lips were also thicker than hers—she had always disliked her thin lips—and they were elegantly outlined against the velvet monotone of his skin.

Tessa noticed with a start that Lucinda was talking again. "I suppose you two have noticed that you sort of look alike," she was saying. It wasn't like Lucinda to make such an awkward remark—nor such an obvious one, Tessa thought. But Lucinda's ex-lover seemed genuinely surprised by her comment. "Really?" he said, looking from Tessa to T.C. curiously. "I don't see it. I mean, how can they possibly look alike when...."

His voice trailed off uneasily, and again there was silence in the little circle. Tessa had just about decided that it was time to take matters into her own hands—although she didn't have the faintest idea how to do it—when T.C. spoke.

"Miss Drew," he said, allowing her to catch the faintest note of bemused complicity beneath his formal tone. "Would you consider joining me out on the deck for a breath of fresh air?"

And he offered his elbow, elegantly crooked, while everyone in their circle stared. Without a word Tessa slipped her hand through his elbow and they walked away.

TESSA WAS SURPRISED to find that the boat had not even left Commercial Wharf. It seemed as if they had been on board for hours. Then she remembered how time had stretched into an eternity while she had been waiting for Lucinda to introduce her to T.C. In fact, the clock on the Customs House tower a few blocks away from the wharf revealed that only thirty minutes had passed since she had stepped aboard. The crew was just beginning to ready the ropes and pull in the gangplank to make ready for the cruise.

Tessa and T.C. looked at each other. So far, they had not spoken two words in private, and Tessa felt an almost palpable urge to start jabbering away. She had no idea what she would say to him—she only knew that it would not be the usual superficial introduction that two strangers normally share. She also knew that if they did not get a chance to be alone together soon, the moment would be lost.

He seemed to feel the same way. He smiled at her, and then nodded in the direction of the gangplank, which was about to be removed.

"Feel like jumping ship?" he murmured. And, without waiting for her answer, he took her hand and moved swiftly forward.

The gangplank was already sliding back against the dock. There was a gap of about three feet where there was nothing but dark water and the murderous thrust of a barnacled piling beneath their feet. But Tessa, as she sailed across that small void to solid land, felt as if she were crossing a huge chasm. Ordinarily, her little imp would be warning her to pause and reconsider. Ordinarily, she would not have jumped off a moving ship with a perfect stranger.

But this was not an ordinary night. It followed a day of surprises—of improbabilities—none of which had registered fully before the next hit her. Douglas's ultimatum, Lucinda's unlikely phone call, her own eerie distance from her emotional reactions—all these contributed to her unusual state of mind and to her sudden decision to follow T.C.'s lead. In fact, as she sailed over three feet of dark and icy water it seemed to be the only logical thing for her to be doing at that moment.

2

ONCE ON SOLID LAND, both Tessa and T.C. broke into grins. "I never was very good at listening to speeches," he confided, taking her hand and linking it through his once again as if they were dear old friends.

"Especially speeches about oneself," Tessa agreed. She was still marveling at how comfortable she felt doing this outrageously impulsive thing. Her little inner voice should have been screaming bloody murder by now. Jumping off a moving boat while holding hands with a complete stranger was not the sort of thing done by a person of common sense. But maybe her little imp was exhausted from the day's emotional strain. Tessa grinned at the absurd mental image.

"What's so funny?" T.C. asked.

"Oh, nothing, really," she replied. "I'm just feeling...funny." She giggled in spite of herself. Tessa would normally have tried to maintain some degree of sophistication when talking to a new acquaintance. But T.C. did not feel like a new acquaintance. And she *was* feeling funny. She felt curiously lightheaded, but quite at ease.

Fortunately, T.C. seemed as comfortable as she was. Tessa was pleased that he made no attempt at

small talk, and that they walked along for long
periods in silence without seeming to care about it.
He exuded a marvelous quality of patience that ap-
pealed to her, especially after Douglas, who seemed
compulsively driven in comparison. Douglas would
never have jumped off a moving boat—he didn't
even leave his apartment in the morning without
having first planned his day down to the second.
Thomas Chimatsu, on the other hand, seemed content to wander along the cobbled sidewalk that led
away from Commercial Wharf and up to Atlantic
Avenue.

Anyway, there was not much that needed to be
discussed. They did not have to bring up the fact of
their physical resemblance. It simply existed, just as
the evening existed, and the salt breeze that lifted
Tessa's thick hair out of the French braid that lay between her shoulder blades. Out of the corner of her
eye she saw that T.C. was smiling at her. Tessa
sighed happily and lifted a stray piece of hair that
had blown across her face. Tonight, she decided, she
would simply let things happen. After all, it was a
stolen evening to begin with.

They had left Commercial Wharf and turned left,
wandering along the pedestrian promenade that led
around picturesque Waterfront Park. To their right,
past the park, Lewis Wharf edged out into the harbor, a luxurious arm of converted warehouses that
contained some of the most desirable living space in
all of Boston.

This section of town was Tessa's favorite. It had
been extensively restored and revitalized to promote

Boston's image as a city with both a past and a future, and had been held up as a paragon of what urban restoration should be like. But Tessa had always found the atmosphere more festive and intimate than impressive and historical. It was like wandering through an ongoing small-town fair. Even on this windy April night, the cobblestoned sidewalks were crowded with people who leaned together into the wind in little groups of two or three, laughing as they walked. The mood of impending spring was infectious, and Tessa smiled and shivered with an odd mixture of apprehension and delight.

"Are you chilled? The night air can get raw this time of year, especially when you're on the water." T.C. slipped her arm more tightly into his as he spoke, and immediately Tessa felt the circle of unspoken intimacy tighten between them. She looked over and saw that he was watching her as if he had been doing so for some time.

"I was pretty chilly before," she admitted, "but I'm fine now. Somehow I don't seem to be feeling the cold." She blushed at the breathless rush of her own words. *What am I saying? This doesn't sound like me at all! It doesn't feel like me, either.* . . . But then, she decided, she hadn't felt like herself all day. At least now she was feeling good.

T.C. laughed, and from the way he ended his laugh with a sympathetic chuckle Tessa wondered if he had any inkling of her inner dialogue. "Being cold is a state of mind, I've always said. If you keep warm thoughts simmering between your ears, you'll have no problem staying toasty."

Well, Tessa thought, she was having no problem coming up with warm thoughts tonight.

"Unfortunately," T.C. went on, "being hungry is not a state of mind. It's a state of emergency and my stomach is growling right now. How about yours?"

"I'm ravenous!" Tessa exclaimed, suddenly realizing that she was.

"Terrific." He stopped on the street and looked around, trying to decide where to go. The wind whipped a strand of dark hair into his eyes and he lifted his free hand to flip it back. His hair was long and thick, and during that moment when it blew over his forehead, he had looked appealingly boyish. "What are you in the mood to eat?" he asked, turning to face her. Despite the boyishness there was something timeless—and very wise—about his eyes.

"I'm in the mood for seafood," she replied promptly. Tessa never had trouble deciding what she wanted to eat—it was reconciling her very definite tastes with her sporadic attempts to stick to a healthy and nonfattening diet that gave her trouble. She adored shellfish, spicy ethnic foods, anything with carbohydrates, and she had a stubbornly untrainable sweet tooth. So far, thanks to years of adolescent sports training, she did not have to worry much about her weight. Still, with her small bones, it was easy to begin to look "soft around the edges," as Tessa called it, especially when the television cameras automatically added on extra pounds.

But tonight she was in no mood to do any monitoring at all. "And pasta," she added as an afterthought. "Definitely pasta."

T.C. grinned and shrugged. "Of course pasta," he confirmed. "Is there any other way to eat seafood?"

"Is there any other way to eat anything?" Tessa inquired, raising her eyebrows in mock astonishment.

T.C. threw back his head and laughed. The sound pealed out over the heads of the crowd, and some people turned to smile at them. T.C. had a wonderful laugh, Tessa decided—full and hearty, as if he was genuinely amused by what she said. She knew she wore a wide grin and wondered if she had underestimated the potency of the wine she had consumed aboard the boat. *Well*, she promised herself, *I'll have something to eat, and then perhaps I'll be able to make some sense out of this evening.*

"You know," said T.C., who had recovered enough to take her arm and start walking again, "I think that statement you just made qualifies as profound. And I happen to know a place in the North End that serves profound linguine."

"Profound linguine, huh?" She leaned into his shoulder as they crossed Atlantic Avenue into the narrow, winding streets that led into the city's famous Italian neighborhood. "Gee, I've never seen that recipe before—what's in it?"

"The chef won't tell...and I don't dare ask," replied T.C. "In this place it's a breach of etiquette to do anything but eat."

Although Tessa was fairly familiar with the North End, she did not recognize the tiny storefront restaurant T.C. led her to. The waitress, however, seemed to know T.C. and waved as she gestured toward a vacant table. She immediately placed a basket of bread and a bottle of chianti on the table without being asked. "How's it going, T.C.?" she inquired casually.

"Are you a regular here?" Tessa asked. She saw that he didn't even bother to consult the menu, which was written on a chalkboard over the kitchen door.

"Actually," said T.C. with a perfectly straight face, "they treat me well because they think I'm half Italian."

Although this was meant to be a joke, and Tessa laughed at the notion that anyone would mistake T.C.'s Eurasian features as Italian, her laugh softened when she realized that it could easily be true. After all, she was half Italian, and they did look alike. She stopped laughing and saw that T.C. was looking at her closely, and that the laugh had faded on his lips, too.

"What's the other half?" she whispered, and they held each other's gaze until the waitress came over to take their order.

They both had linguine with clam sauce, and Tessa applauded T.C. on his choice. The linguine, she decided, was profound, there was no other word for it. Then they split an order of mussels marinara and moved their chairs closer together so that they could lift the plump delicate shellfish from the same steaming bowl. All the while they drank chianti as if it were grape juice and were so busy talking and eating that the wine seemed to have little effect.

"Tell me the truth," Tessa said, "what did you really think when you found out you won the Boston Best award for the Elliott Sanctuary?"

T.C. shrugged. "Mostly I felt embarrassed, I suppose. I've always had a pretty condescending attitude about things like that—you know, awards, honors, that sort of stuff. It's mostly chamber-of-commerce-type publicity, not really an indication of skills."

"I agree," Tessa said. "It's mostly hype, isn't it?"

T.C. grinned sheepishly. "To be perfectly frank, Tessa, I was embarrassed because I felt so damned proud of myself for winning, do you believe it?"

Tessa giggled. "I felt exactly the same way—isn't that awful?" She made a swift gesture in the air with her fork and a bit of tomato dropped back into the bowl. "I guess I wanted to think of myself as being above such crass promotional schemes, but when the letter came, I wanted to print it on a banner for everyone to see. I was so embarrassed at—"

T.C. leaned closer and flicked something off her cheek. "Tomato," he informed her, and then he put the tip of his finger into his mouth.

Something about this tiny gesture stopped Tessa's chatter cold. On the surface, T.C. appeared to be listening to her with every indication of absorption. But the deliberate eroticism with which he drew the tiny fleck of tomato from her cheek to his mouth, and the slow, sensual circle that his tongue made around the perimeter of his lips made Tessa forget entirely what she had been about to say. She could only watch as his eyes turned subtly greener, and his whole body grew so still that she wondered how his heart could be beating at all. Hers was, she knew, and loudly.

"Tomato," she repeated, and felt her throat tightening around the word. She was aware of the

warmth of arousal spreading along her belly and
thighs, and she was vaguely annoyed at herself. *Hey,*
she wanted to say, *hang on there a minute. This is
not supposed to be happening—not tonight, not after
today and certainly not here in this two-by-four restaurant.* She suddenly longed for her usual sensible
perspective. But the inner voice refused to come to
her rescue. There was no one to argue the other side,
so Tessa could do nothing but watch as the green
light slowly receded from T.C.'s eyes and his body
relaxed.

The entire episode could not have taken more than
thirty seconds, and then they resumed their conversation as if nothing extraordinary had happened at
all. But Tessa knew something had shifted. Later on,
when she relived that night, she would remember this
moment and decide that this had been her point of no
return.

They finished their meal and wandered for a while
down the main street of the North End.

"Where to?" Tessa inquired lightly. She hardly
knew what she wanted the answer to be.

T.C. looked at her quizzically, and Tessa, who did
not ordinarily blush, did so for the second time that
evening. He had an uncanny habit of seeming to
know her innermost thoughts. But T.C. only grinned
and shrugged. "To dessert," he said. "Where else
does a normal human being go after a huge meal of
pasta, seafood and wine?"

Tessa laughed and sent up a silent prayer of thanks
to the sweet-tooth fairy for not having to suggest it
herself. "Most normal human beings would head for

the emergency room after consuming what we did just now," she said. "But I never said I was normal."

"No," T.C. observed, "you didn't. You never had to say a word." The look of complicity that passed between them at that moment was as palpable as a caress.

Then, suddenly, they were in front of a tiny pastry shop, its bowed window frosted over with steam. A sugary warmth emanated from the doorway in the form of a beckoning aroma. Once again the spell had been broken. Tessa was not sure whether she was frustrated or relieved.

The shop was even tinier than the restaurant had been, and was filled with people gathered around minuscule wrought-iron tables with marble tops. The service counter was almost completely obscured by a huge silver espresso machine.

"That looks like something straight out of *Star Wars*, doesn't it?" T.C. said.

"And it smells like something straight out of this galaxy," replied Tessa, breathing in deeply.

"The combination of strong coffee and sweets is one of the most powerful narcotics known to man," T.C. reported in a scholarly tone as he led Tessa to a tiny window seat. "To woman, too, of course."

Tessa laughed. "Is that another of your theories?"

"Not theory, my dear," he told her. "Pure scientific fact. I should know. I'm the biggest dessert addict in the world."

"Wanna bet?" Their order arrived, and Tessa picked up her pastry and bit into it with a challenging grin.

They ate crisp, fragrant almond buns and drank the strong espresso, twisting around in their seats to watch the parade of passersby. They spoke casually, commenting on what they saw and heard. Then they lapsed once again into silence.

But this time it was different. T.C.'s effect on Tessa had been very strong, even allowing for the fact that she was in an unusually impressionable state of mind. Suddenly, silence was not enough. Now she wanted to know more about the strange mirror-image man who sat beside her. She felt she had known him forever, yet she knew nothing about him. Somewhere just behind her conscious thoughts lay the conviction that Thomas Chimatsu was going to play an important part in her life, and she wanted to know who he was.

T.C. seemed to be aware of the change in her mood because he was watching her with a patient, quizzical smile on his face. "You were saying . . . ?" he began encouragingly.

She had not been saying, but she knew what he meant and decided to go right to the heart of the matter. "Who are you, Thomas Chimatsu? Where did you come from?"

On any other night, this would have sounded incredibly rude to Tessa herself, not to mention the effect such forthrightness would have had on the other party. But this was not any other night—and not any other man. T.C. nodded as if the questions were exactly what he had been expecting. He took a last sip of his espresso and then, after placing the cup down carefully, spread his hands out flat on the table as if inviting Tessa's inspection.

"My name is Thomas Chimatsu," he said in a soft, clear voice. "I'm an environmental architect with Sullivan and Floyd, in Cambridge. I was born in London, but grew up all over the world, and came to the States when I was twelve. My father is Japanese, but he was brought up in England. My mother is half English, half Irish—" T.C. broke off his monologue and smiled "—like you, actually."

"How did you know I was half Irish?" Tessa asked.

The smile erupted into a chuckle. "Where else would you get eyes so much like mine?"

Tessa pursed her lips, then grinned. "From the Italian side, I would have guessed." They laughed together for a moment, until T.C. saw Tessa's smile disappear.

"What is it?" he inquired gently.

She shook her head, more in wonder than in denial. "It's very strange, isn't it?" she said in a hushed voice. "I mean, that we look so much alike. Don't you find it strange?"

T.C. reached down into her lap and took one of her hands, which he placed gently on the table. Then he laid his hand beside it. Tessa looked down at their fingers spread side by side—hers long and narrow, his strong and surprisingly wide for a smallish man. "I don't find it strange at all," he said. "I find it rather magical." He picked up her hand, placed it on top of his, and then placed his free hand over it. "Now," he said. "Your turn. Who are you, Tessa Drew?" He smiled encouragingly.

Tessa shrugged. It was not as easy for her to recite her past as it had apparently been for him. Besides, she was aware of a growing confusion, as if the spell of comfort and confidence that T.C. had spun around her might be wearing off.

"Well, mine isn't a very exciting life," she began. "I grew up in a suburb of Chicago and went to Northwestern University as a print journalism major. Then I switched to television and went to Baltimore to do an internship with a station there." Baltimore. Tessa paused and waited for a catch to form in her throat at the mention of the city. Nothing. She took a deep breath and went on. "That's all, really. I lived in the same house all my life until I moved into the dorm at Northwestern, and then I was still only an hour from home. I didn't really feel like I was on my own until I moved here four years ago to take the job with Channel 8." Her voice trailed off into a whisper. "I'm not even sure I'm on my own now." She was thinking of her inner voice. T.C., she noticed, was watching her closely, so she laughed to dispel the sudden tension. "I guess we couldn't have come from more different backgrounds if we had planned it, huh?" She looked away nervously.

"It would have been impossible to plan it," he said, keeping his eyes steadily on hers. Then he reached out and lifted her chin, turning her face toward his. He cradled her chin gently between his thumb and forefinger and drew her closer to him. In that long moment, as they gazed into each other's eyes, Tessa became aware that the mood in the sweet shop had changed. It was getting late, and the crowds of patrons at the marble tables had gone. The ovens and the espresso machine had been turned off, and steam no longer obscured the window. She looked out on the street and saw that the festive strollers had begun to walk more quickly, bundled up against the wind, obviously headed home. She felt momentarily lost, staring out into the dark.

But when she looked back at T.C., she felt calmed again by the patience she saw on his face. Once again his free hand moved to her face, but this time to brush a long caress along the length of her cheek.

"Tessa," he said, whispering her name like a lullaby. "I see you trying to make decisions, and I don't think tonight is a time for decisions, do you?"

For a moment she wondered what he was talking about. She *hadn't* been trying to make any decisions and wouldn't have been able to even if she had tried. Then she realized what he was saying and, simultaneously, what her heart had been trying to say to her all evening.

She shook her head, both to ward off the certainty of her own feelings and to deny his statement. "Oh, no," she began. "I'm not . . . I don't want . . . ."

"Shhhh." His fingers slipped around to brush against her lips. Tessa pulled away, momentarily annoyed that he had had such a clear view into feelings that she herself had not been aware of.

"Really," she began, but he had already removed his hand and stood up.

"I have an idea," he said, smiling down at her. "I haven't been to the Aquarium in ages. I'd love to take you there—tomorrow." His voice dropped slightly, and Tessa was aware of a tiny edge of vulnerability that she had not heard before. "Are you free tomorrow afternoon, Tessa—around one?"

She sat very still, looking up at him, wondering for the umpteenth time that day how she should respond. Of course she should tell him that she was sorry but she would be busy tomorrow. After all, she did have certain unfinished business—namely Douglas, who had probably been trying to reach her all evening. Besides, the evening hadn't really progressed to her satisfaction. She had wanted something more on this stolen night. If she was going to throw her lot in with the impulsive people of the world, Tessa Drew intended to do it in a big way.

It was all in her own hands. She could accept the date. She could turn him down. Or she could suggest that they go home together right away. Tessa tried to read the message behind his eyes, but they had become impenetrable mirrors of her own. He was not going to read her mind for her on this one.

Once again, her instincts came to the rescue. "I hear there's a great new trained-seal act there," she said at last, forcing a grin and wondering what had made her say that.

T.C. let out his breath in an odd little sigh, then smiled and held out his hand. "Let's get you a cab," he said.

Tessa allowed him to steer her out the door and onto the curb then usher her inside a taxi. Just as he was pulling his head out of the cab, he leaned forward. "It's right," he whispered against her ear, his voice surprisingly ragged. "It's just not right tonight, Tessa. See you tomorrow."

And he was gone, leaving Tessa to wonder if his odd little sigh had been one of relief or regret. And whether tomorrow would be right for them, after all.

3

TESSA WAS EARLY for her date with T.C. At twelve-forty-five she walked slowly through Haymarket and Faneuil Hall on her way to the Aquarium, but the day was raw and gray, and she could find no excuse to linger out of doors. She was never early for anything, she told herself, and she didn't want to mislead Thomas Chimatsu by having him think that she was a prompt individual.

The truth was that she had been ready since early Sunday morning. She had come home fully expecting not to sleep a wink. After all, between Douglas and T.C. she had so much to ponder she might never sleep again! But she had fallen immediately into a deep and restful slumber and had gotten up early that morning eager for only one thing—to see T.C. again.

Normally, Tessa thought to herself as she approached the broad brick terrace that marked the entrance to the Aquarium, mornings were supposed to bring sanity and clarity of thought. She should have awakened full of remorse about Douglas, and fully aware that her evening with Thomas Chimatsu had been nothing more than a momentary aberration due to suppressed emotional stress. She should have awakened with a pounding headache from all that chianti, not to mention a stomachache from all that food, and certainly a deep sense of shock at having jumped across a three-foot abyss with a perfect stranger.

Instead, she took an hour-long soak in a perfumed tub and spent another hour deciding what to wear. She finally decided on a cobalt-blue silk blouse and a crisp white cotton skirt with navy sling-back shoes.

The simple truth was she liked T.C. a lot. She liked being with him, talking to him and the fact that they seemed to have so much in common. The fact that he was so satisfying to look at didn't hurt either, even if Tessa was aware of a tiny egotistical twist to her attraction for him. She felt comfortable and daring at the same time.

And this morning she forgave him for being a bit manipulative last night. After all, last night she had been in no shape to make any clear decisions, and going home with a perfect stranger would certainly have been a mistake.

Today he was no longer a stranger. Tessa walked faster in spite of her desire not to appear overeager. But then, just as she rounded the corner that opened on to the terrace of the Aquarium, she caught sight of someone leaning over a railing at the far end of the open space, and her heart caught against her ribs. All she saw was the back of an unfamiliar black raincoat, but she did not have to look twice to be sure who it was. She broke into a rapid stride. T.C. turned around and watched her approach.

"You're early," he said, making the statement sound like the highest of compliments.

"So are you," she replied. For a moment they both grinned in silence. It occurred to Tessa that T.C. might not have been certain she would show up. She was glad the same thought had not occurred to her.

"Look at this." T.C. turned back to the railing and Tessa stepped up beside him. Below her was a small, kidney-shaped, shallow pool. Lolling in the water were four huge walruses, obviously enjoying the attention they were receiving from the strange creatures up above. "This one is Stanley, that one is Harold and the other one over there is Ralph."

"How do you know?"

"They told me, of course."

"Oh, really? I didn't know you spoke walrus," Tessa said.

T.C. looked at Tessa in amazement. "You don't believe me? How else would I know their names? Listen." He turned back to the railing and leaned farther over the edge. "What's your name?" he said in a singsong voice to the nearest animal. "What's your name?"

The walrus nearest to T.C. gave a low belch that sounded to Tessa remarkably like the name Ralph. She burst into a peal of laughter.

"I told you they gave me their names," T.C. said triumphantly.

"But you said he was Stanley!" Tessa hooted.

T.C. managed to look wounded and dubious at the same time. "They must have switched places while my back was turned," he muttered. "Walruses are sneaky."

"Who's the fourth one over there?" asked Tessa.

"Or haven't you been introduced?" She looped her arm through his and leaned against him to point to the far end of the pool. It occurred to her that, right from the start, there had been no physical awkwardness between them. They fit together so well, so naturally. She liked the solid warmth of his shoulder pressing against her chin, especially since the wind off the water was so bitter.

"That one? That's the she-walrus," T.C. replied. "At least I think it's the she-walrus."

Tessa giggled, looking at the fat, sleek animal. "How can you tell?"

"I can tell," he said slowly, "because she's the only one who's not talking. And because I can't take my eyes off her."

Tessa chuckled and turned to him to make a smart comment, but stopped when she caught the serious look on T.C.'s face. "I don't—she-walruses aren't usually so reticent," she faltered, then abandoned all pretense at wit. She could feel the power of his warm gaze drawing her face closer to his.

"I've never met one quite like this before," T.C. whispered. His voice was like a kiss, and suddenly Tessa knew that the time, though unexamined and unexplained, was exactly right.

Later on, she would try to remember what on earth she had expected to happen between T.C. and herself on that rainy Sunday afternoon. Had she really expected they would stroll through the Aquarium with all the families and teenagers gawking at the shark tank and laughing on cue at the antics of the trained seals? She could not have been that naive!

Yet she was unable to comprehend how that gray afternoon had, quickly and without a moment's warning, turned into an encounter fraught with such emotional tension. Surely the other walrus watchers around the pool had not been similarly affected. Surely they must all be aware of the sexual energy radiating from her and T.C. in concentric circles, like ripples in a lake.

It was unexplainable—another unexplainable event in a life that had, up until twenty-four hours ago, been clear and well-planned. But Tessa had no intention of arguing with her inner voice now, even if her little imp had been around to argue.

T.C. was speaking and Tessa watched his lips move as if mesmerized by the motion. "She would only give me one piece of information, that she-walrus," he said.

"What was that?" Tessa held her breath.

"She told me," he said, with an inviting half smile, "that the trained-seal show is not worth waiting around for."

Tessa grinned slowly. "There's not much that is," she said. "Worth waiting for."

"Well," said Thomas, tucking her arm under his and turning away from the railing. "We'll see about that."

They crossed the terrace, leaning together into the wind and mist. Tessa was conscious of how closely their steps matched, of how their shoulders, arms and hips all came into contact with one another at exactly the right point for maximum comfort. But there was more than comfort to their physical connection this time. Things had changed, and now their physical connection had become charged with a new kind of energy—the expectant charge of desire about to be fulfilled.

Tessa had no idea where T.C. lived, but she followed his steps as if of the same mind. She felt a hush of anticipation fill her soul, and she was unnaturally attuned to every nuance of his body. Whatever doubts she had felt about T.C.—or about the idea of rushing into a relationship with a near-stranger— were laid to rest as she watched his intense, strongly familiar profile against the gray light of the afternoon. This was right—for a lot of reasons. And he was no longer a stranger to her.

Her musing was interrupted when T.C. turned unexpectedly down a stone-paved walkway and Tessa, looking up, realized where they were. "This is Lewis Wharf!" She looked at T.C. "You live at Lewis Wharf?"

T.C. inserted a key in the elevator door and smiled. "Somebody has to," he said solemnly.

Tessa had to grin at his drollery. "Poor you," she commiserated. "You have to live in the most exciting restoration project in the city."

T.C. raised his eyebrows in amusement. The elevator doors opened and they got off four floors up, on the top floor of the redesigned warehouse. Tessa found herself standing in a tiny hallway that was obviously T.C.'s private entry. The walls were covered with a grass cloth that gave off a faintly woodsy smell. Light filtered through antique smoked-glass sconces on two of the walls and reflected an amber glow off the polished black slate floor. A brass urn in one corner held a tall spray of bulrushes and cattails, and an Oriental silk print in cinnabar and royal blue added a vibrant touch. The effect was both tasteful and serene.

T.C. moved ahead of Tessa to open the black door that faced them. She swallowed and realized she was holding her breath again. She felt fragile and tense, as if she were a bird poised for flight. But she was quite certain that she did not want to fly away.

"Welcome to my home," T.C. said, and his easy smile flooded Tessa with joy. Behind him, the door swung open to reveal a wide expanse of seemingly empty space. Tessa eagerly stepped past him into the room.

"This is incredible!" She stood in the middle of the room and turned slowly around. "Do all the apartments in Lewis Wharf look like this?"

"I knocked down a few walls when I bought the place," he said. He gestured eloquently at the four walls. "I tore them all down, as a matter of fact."

Tessa was standing in a room that at first looked totally devoid of color. Everything—the walls, the floor, the low furniture—seemed to blend together in a remarkably liquid shade of gray-beige. The ceiling stretched up two stories and ended in a skylight that was filled with the dusky tones of evening. The walls were bleached brick, warmed with soft lighting and a few delicate prints. Glass sliding doors ran the entire length of one wall, covered in a filmy open-weave fabric that reminded Tessa of old lace. Even the steel-gray sky glimpsed through the fabric matched the general tone of serenity and calm.

Two camel-backed chaise lounges, covered in deep plum-colored fabric and strewn with plump pillows, stood at right angles in front of a wood-burning stove in one corner, and in another a thick, feathery-looking mattress lay on a raised platform. Bleached wooden shutters hid what Tessa imagined must be the kitchen and bathroom areas, and a wrought-iron staircase spiraled up to a loft under the skylight.

Tessa thought of her own apartment in a narrow brick town house in Boston's South End. The rooms were warm and cozy but they were packed full of the memorabilia of her active life. A haphazard collection of antiques mingled with furniture that she had been living with since college, narrow turreted window seats stuffed with books and pillows, and a collection of poster art that assailed the eyes. By comparison, this space seemed like a haven of simplicity, and Tessa understood why she had been unable to sort things out during these past few days. She had needed silent space.

She felt something start to unwind deep in the pit of her stomach, and she sighed with relief and delight. "It's so...I don't know...it's so...."

"You mean it's so obviously Japanese, don't you?"

Tessa looked up, wondering if he had taken offense. But T.C.'s dark eyes were bright with humor, and he offered her a demure bow from the waist while he chuckled.

"That's exactly what I meant, Mr. Chimatsu," she laughed.

He nodded. "That's usually the impression this place gives," he went on. "Although I didn't really intend that. I'm sure some elements of Oriental design went into my plans, but that wasn't the point. My father was a vice-consul for the Japanese embassy—I told you we moved around a lot when I was growing up. Perhaps I just naturally learned to make do with fewer things. It's sort of an inbred aversion to clutter, I guess, even though I've been living here for several years and have no intention of ever moving again."

Tessa pursed her lips thoughtfully. "I was born and raised in the same place—the same house. I had the same bedroom set for thirteen years." She closed her eyes briefly to conjure more clearly the image of her childhood home. "You can collect a lot of junk spending eighteen years in the same room."

She opened her eyes, smiling, but found that T.C. was watching her intently. "What are you looking at?" she asked.

"Us," he replied in a hushed tone. He stepped forward and lifted his hand as if to touch her cheek, then stopped just short of contact. Instinctively turning her head toward the gesture, Tessa caught sight of the two of them, mirrored against the flat opaque gray sky through a stretch of uncurtained glass wall. Their features were blurred so that, for an instant, it looked to Tessa as if she and T.C. were exact shadowy replicas of each other. Not their real selves, which stood motionless in the spacious room, but their mirrored images hanging out there in the sky. It was their images that were twins.

Tessa took an involuntary step back. A silence had

filled the room as liquid fills a bowl. In that silence Tessa thought suddenly of Douglas Bright. Douglas made his life out of words, just as she did. This man before her, T.C., made his life out of spaces. Despite their identical images, wavering in the gray light of the waning afternoon, Tessa knew this to be the deepest difference between them.

Somehow she felt she should reveal more of herself to T.C. before they became lovers—as he should to her. She knew she should use words to explain to him what was happening in her life, since he now seemed to be so inextricably tied up in it. He had been right last night—the reasons for being together—intimately— had not been there. What, then, made it so right at this moment?

But Tessa was in no mood to deal with words. Words were the bread and butter of her daily life. Not only did she make her living by them, she also lived by them. If anything, she lived too much by the head and not enough by the heart and instinct.

Today, though—today she wanted only to deal in spaces, big and silent spaces that eased her mind. She wanted to throw herself into that cool, clear pool of space that T.C. reflected back at her when she looked at him. The fact that there might be many things behind his smile that she did not yet understand was unimportant. Today she needed to clear her mind of all preconceptions and slip into that pool of desire.

He was waiting, but she could see the glow in his eyes, the fires banked until he commanded them forth. She gestured toward the wall of glass. "Today feels right, T.C.," she whispered. "We're all that matters today—us, and those two out there."

T.C. reached out and pulled on a cord, and the lacy curtains drew completely shut, cutting off the misty image. "There is no them," he said. "There's only us. And it's right for us...oh, yes, it's right." He gave a little groan as he stepped closer to her and lifted his hands, bringing them down gently on either side of her head. Slowly, he brought his fingers down the silky wash of her hair, his face searching hers hungrily. When his fingers reached her neck, they rested for a moment on the throbbing pulse of her throat. Then his lips came forward and rested against hers. It was the first time their lips had met.

It was a light touch, like the wings of a butterfly coming to rest on a flower. Tessa leaned into it, eager to taste his mouth with hers. Despite the delicacy of his touch, she could feel the strength of his fingers supporting her nape, and she was aware of the controlled tension in his body. His thumbs roamed delicately over the contours of her face, coming to rest on the crest of Tessa's high cheekbones. She felt her body warming, melting under this simple touch.

"You have such marvelous hands," she murmured.

"And you," he whispered, "you have a face like a valentine."

The grace of his comment, delivered in a voice deepened by desire, sent a shiver down Tessa's spine and her limbs quivered in anticipation. "You're shivering, valentine. Come with me here while I build us a fire." T.C. took her hand, which was cold and dry, in his warm one and led her over to the wood stove. He knelt and began to prepare the kindling and wood for the blaze. Tessa stood there, entranced by the grace and economy of his movement. He seemed to think before every move he made, and then once he moved it was with a strength that revealed absolute confidence. Her entire body tingled and she felt weak with the longing for those sure, gentle hands.

At last the flames leaped up in the belly of the barrel-shaped stove, and Thomas stood up letting the warmth and light flow around him into the room. Instinctively, Tessa held her hands out toward him, and toward the blaze. He took her hands again and turned them over several times as if examining her narrow fingers against the wider expanse of his own. Then he slowly lifted one of his hands and laid it against her cheek with an achingly light touch. Tessa trembled and leaned into his fingers. Then he lifted her hand and laid it against his smooth jaw.

Immediately, as if she had been instructed to do so, Tessa was aware of the difference between her own soft, rather cool skin and his—warmer and slightly rougher, but still smooth. Then T.C. began to move his fingers across the high plane of her cheek and across her lips. She did the same to his, exploring his features as he did hers, like perfect mirror images.

It never occurred to Tessa that what they did might be a result of their mutual fascination with their resemblance. To her, what she and Thomas Chimatsu discovered that afternoon was simply the most erotic experience of their lives. There was nothing kinky about it, only a sense of wonder and awe that his body should be so beautiful, and that hers should react to his in such complete harmony. She felt some long-forgotten passion opening up inside her like a late-blooming flower.

Still, they had not really kissed. Now, when their mouths finally met, it was like a slow-motion explosion. She heard T.C. groan against her lips, and she felt her knees buckle. They slipped together to the floor, mouths locked in an embrace that seemed unbreachable. Tessa was intensely aware of every sound in the near-silent room. There was a hiss and crackle as the logs settled into the burning grate, and a distant thud from some construction project on Lewis Wharf. But other than that she was unaware of the outside world and of the passage of time.

But soon T.C. was no longer content. He pulled away and looked at her, his eyes warm with desire. "I need more of you," he whispered, running his hands down her sides. "Shall we take off our clothes now?" It seemed the most natural question in the world to be asking—and the most natural to answer.

"Of course."

"Do you want to use the other room?"

She smiled at his sudden delicacy and shook her head. "No," she replied. "I want to stay here—with you."

T.C. nodded gravely and kissed her. Then he turned and pulled a quilt off one of the couches. It was made of satin and slithered to the floor around them in a hiss that sounded like the fire. That done, he lifted his hands to the top button of Tessa's silk shirt. Again, as if responding to a silent cue, Tessa did the same with his.

They began undressing each other, still moving at the same stately almost ceremonial pace. But now the room became filled with a mounting tension. Again and again, as they slipped articles of clothing from each other's body, Tessa's breath caught, or her face flushed with a sudden onset of desire. She could see that the same thing was happening to T.C. from the way his eyes glittered like dark coals in his tanned face, or from the way he suddenly pressed his lips together as he watched her body revealed before him.

When her breasts came free of her camisole—small but well-rounded in the half-light—she heard a sharp intake of breath and saw T.C. shudder and make a fist to keep from reaching out for her until they were done. But the intake of breath had been her own, because his eyes caressed her nipples so palpably that they sprang erect at once under his hungry gaze.

She wanted to close her eyes to avert the overpowering waves of arousal, to stave them off until she could regain some control over her body, but she could not risk missing a moment of revelation. She was too hungry for T.C. to have any shame, or any control.

At last they were both undressed, and T.C. stood revealed before her. The firelight flooded his back so that it seemed, at first glance, that his body vibrated with heat. He was beautifully proportioned, with strong, clearly outlined muscles that glided over his frame without bulging. His skin looked a mellow amber color, shot into gold by the light of the fire.

There was little hair on his body, except where his
groin melted into shadow. Tessa felt the tension con-
stricting her breath, and now she had to look away.
She looked down at her own body, which also seemed
to vibrate, and then back to T.C.'s erect desire. The
time had come when she could dance his dance of
arousal no longer. She met his eyes and nodded almost
imperceptibly. But T.C. was spinning their sensations
out even longer.

"You are an exquisite creature," T.C. sighed rag-
gedly, and he reached out to touch one pointed
breast and then the other. Tessa thought she could
fall into his fingers, but she kept upright by losing
herself in the fires of his eyes. Her flesh, already
warmed, was inflamed by his butterfly caresses, and
she could feel her loins melting into moisture. She
drank in his ardent gaze as if it would dampen her in-
ternal fires, but it only aroused her further.

Then, just when she thought she would scream
out with desire, T.C. uttered a low growl and pulled
her roughly against him. Their mouths met with
ravenous ferocity and their limbs locked as if compelled by a magnetic force. There was, even in their
arousal, the exactitude of perfect fit. It felt like coming home.

T.C. lay back on the quilt, pulling her over him
and holding her up with a gentle, caressing grasp
around her ribs. Her legs folded in between his, and
she could feel him growing even harder than before
against her thighs. His hair fell back from his forehead in thick, silky strands, and hers fell over her
shoulders onto his chest, mingling with his as neatly

as if it had been his own. His face was glowing with the effort of containment, but still he did not enter her. Instead, he settled her around him and surveyed her flushed features with a half smile. Tessa had never been played so expertly before, like a string that has been stretched to the breaking point, yet still quivers at a high pitch of intensity. At this point, even his gaze was so arousing that she dared not meet it fully. If T.C. was waiting for their fires to recede somewhat, he waited in vain, she thought.

"As soon as you stepped onto that boat," T.C. whispered hoarsely, "I imagined being with you like this."

Tessa, who had not imagined herself capable of speech, was startled by this admission. "You did?" He had not seemed to her, at the time, the type of man who would engage in erotic fantasies about strangers. "I had no idea."

T.C. chuckled. "I would have been completely embarrassed if you had guessed what I was thinking." He lifted his head just high enough to place a lingering kiss between the valley of her breasts. Then he let his head fall back with another throaty sigh. "If you could guess what I'm thinking now," he began but Tessa cut him off.

"I don't need to guess, damn you," she hissed, dipping her head so that her tongue could flick across his chest. "I just need to feel you inside me—now."

Like a tiger with its prey, T.C. roughly pulled her to him. His lips sprang hungrily to her mouth, forcing it open so that his tongue could dart deep inside. At the same time he parted her thighs, maneuvering

her hips so that he could enter her at the point of
greatest sensation.

He need not have bothered. Tessa was all sensation, and his touch galvanized every nerve in her
body into a maelstrom of delights. Her feet tangled
with his and her hair raked like heavy silk across his
chest as she moved astride him. She felt ignited from
above and below, and the heat was becoming
molten, threatening to explode at any moment.

But T.C., with uncanny skill, regulated the fire. He
moved her above him as if she were weightless, re-
adjusting his body and hers to meet at the most in-
flammable points, then pulling back so that they
could savor the ecstasy, just as the wave of flame
threatened to overtake them. Tessa had only to think
about the possibility of an improvement on their
positions for it to happen. Their two bodies, only
slightly similar in reality, had become, at this moment of heightened awareness, two sides of the same
coin. They moved as one.

Then T.C.'s hands gripped her buttocks and he
rolled above her, stretching backward so that her
legs, twined about his waist, lifted up in an arc,
touched by the fire's light. Now they began to move
more rapidly, as if the cue had been given at last.

The moment before the explosion, Tessa was
aware of sounds in the room, her senses heightened
by approaching climax. The sounds, she knew, came
from T.C. and herself, but there was another sound;
the room seemed to be filling up with a low humming
sound that grew louder and louder, just as the topaz
light from the fire grew brighter and brighter. It

seemed as if the very space their bodies inhabited was creating the sound and the light, and Tessa wondered if the crescendo could go on forever. She thought she could bear it no longer and cried out just as the sound and light and sensation reached a peak. There was one long, drawn-out shower of ecstasy, and then Tessa felt herself falling deeply, easily, into the warm, still waters of her lover's reflecting gaze.

THE FIRE WAS LOW and the afternoon had faded into evening by the time they stirred. The room was washed in shadows and quiet at last, but Tessa knew she had to speak. She had inhabited a world of space and silence with T.C., and the experience had been unlike any she had ever known. But now, as they lay together in the wordless communication of total satiation, she knew she must somehow return to her own reality, to the reality of words. A part of her brain—was it her inner voice making a belated appearance—told her that her connection with T.C. went deeper than pure physical attraction, because that alone could not have accounted for the ecstasy they had just shared. But she felt she owed it to both of them to explain to T.C. where she was coming from and where she stood. And she owed it to Douglas, too, in all fairness. Her sense of honesty and fair play was too great to let this moment go unexplained.

"Wait."

Before Tessa could say a word, T.C. reached up his arm from where it lay behind her neck and dropped two fingers on her lips. "You don't have to say anything just yet."

Tessa twisted her head around to stare at him. "What makes you so sure I was going to say anything?" she asked, feeling instantly guilty.

He smiled and dropped a kiss on the top of her head. "Your brain was clanking away. I could hear wheels turning." He made a comical whirring sound between his teeth.

Tessa shrugged, but his uncanny perception left her slightly nonplussed. "I just wanted to tell you . . . ." She stopped herself this time. What did she want to tell him? Surely it would be inappropriate to tell T.C. about Douglas right now, regardless of how incredibly close she had felt to him moments ago.

On the other hand, Tessa didn't want him to get the wrong impression about what kind of person she was, or about her future plans. She knew better than to imagine that he thought she made a habit of going to bed with strangers, but she didn't want him to think she expected this to be the start of something long-term. After all, her life was still up in the air, and Tessa still felt that at some point she would have to deal with the loss of Douglas. The one thing she did not need was an impetuously wrought commitment to someone else.

"Look," she began, pulling herself into a sitting position and turning around to face him.

He lay on his back, his arms clasped behind his head. The sharp angle of his elbow made his biceps bulge appealingly, and Tessa gazed abstractly at the smooth tawny expanse of skin that flowed into the slightly damp hollow of his armpits.

When she looked at his face she saw he was grinning. The grin made his face look less serious and more impish, especially since that heavy lock of hair had once again fallen across his forehead. She reached out and brushed it aside. Maybe the words should wait.

"You were saying?" he inquired blithely.

"I was saying. . . ." She grinned back at him and shook her head. "I wasn't saying much of anything, was I?"

"Not so far."

Tessa decided to try again, from a different angle. "Look, T.C., last night and today have been. . .well, wonderful. . . ."

"But?" He did not seem concerned, even as he supplied the qualifying conjunction.

"But. . .well, look, I'm not used to doing this sort of thing. I mean, I admit there's something pretty unusual about you and me, but. . .well, the point is, we have to realize we still don't know each other very well. And we should be careful of getting too involved, shouldn't we?"

"I haven't the faintest idea if we should or not."

"You don't?"

"Of course I don't. How could anybody? We just met, we're still strangers, and it's not later yet. How could we possibly know how we'll feel later when it's still now? And give me back some covers, please."

He pulled gently on the quilt and Tessa helped him fling one corner over his exposed thigh. She doggedly continued, "What I meant was that. . .well, there's been a lot going on in my life lately—as of twenty-four hours ago, to be exact, and I feel I should let you know that I have some issues to work out—something to do with my past."

She stopped, surprised. She hadn't realized until that moment that she was thinking about Douglas in the past tense. Was it really that simple, then? Was that all she had to do to dismiss three years of her life and what she thought had been a serious commitment? No, it couldn't be that simple. She had never trusted simple solutions.

T.C. was looking at her with that same faintly challenging air of knowing exactly what she was thinking.

"Am I making any sense?" she asked him suddenly.

He grinned. "Not a bit. But you're reading your lines perfectly. Don't let me interrupt."

"Hey, let's not get too flippant about this. I'm trying to explain something to you—"

"And I'm telling you not to bother. Please." His voice was unexpectedly gentle and serious, and Tessa settled back among the covers to let him speak. "Listen, Tessa. What I mean is, this scenario is not necessary. I appreciate your attempt at honesty. God knows my track record is not that great when it comes to certain commitments either." Tessa started to interrupt, to ask him how in the world he had known she was talking about commitments, but he stopped her. "I also appreciate your attempts to put this strange and wonderful experience we've just shared into some kind of perspective, if such a thing is possible. I have a constant urge to do that kind of cataloging too. But all I'm saying now is to let it alone for a bit. It doesn't have to mean anything at all, what happened with us."

Tessa felt a stab of disappointment at this remark. Was *that* what he thought it meant? Certainly *she* had not meant that their time together was meaningless. But he was still talking.

"Or it can mean something very special. But you don't have to think about the future tonight, just like you don't have to think about the past. There's only right now—and all this." He reached out and swept his arm around the room, resting fondly on her shoulder.

Tessa smiled and leaned into his hand. "Now *that* sounds obviously Oriental—like some eastern philosophy."

He laughed. "It is. But it's true. Because if this is the start of the rest of our lives, as they say in those vitamin commercials, then we have plenty of time to sort out past, present and future. And if it's not. . . ." He used his fingers to urge her back down with him on the floor. "Well, if it's not, then we'd better make the best of what we've got, don't you agree?"

Tessa snuggled against him. She could not tell which alternative he favored, if any. But what he said suited her perfectly for now. "I couldn't agree more," she said firmly.

"Good. Then you'll stay the night, won't you?" He began to drop tiny kisses along her face and neck. "I wish you would."

"I'd be delighted." Tessa snuggled into the crook of his arm, feeling a great sense of relief. She felt she had been given a reprieve. T.C. was right. Either she would sort out her life later, or she would not sort it out at all. That possibility was truly liberating. In either case, none of it had to do with T.C., or tonight. "Can I just ask you one silly question?" she inquired, twisting her head up so that she spoke against the underside of his chin.

"You can try. I suspect you've rarely asked a silly question—but give it a whirl."

Tessa bit her lip. The question had been on her mind all evening, but she had not allowed herself to even think about it. After all, she disliked being asked that kind of question herself. And besides, the coincidence would be just too great. But tonight was a night for throwing better judgment to the winds, so she shut her eyes against the fragrant thrust of his jaw and rushed the words out. "What's your astrological sign?"

His laugh pealed out into the room like a burst of sunlight. Then he lifted himself up and tucked her body more firmly to his, smoothing the quilt out around them again so that their bare flanks were exposed to the warmth of the wood stove. "I'm a Gemini, of course," he said, bending to caress one nipple between his even teeth.

Tessa caught her breath, partly at what he had said, and partly at the rush of sensation that flooded up from her chest and down into her loins. "So am I," she breathed. "I'm a Gemini, too!"

T.C. raised himself up and slid into her with exquisite control. "What," he murmured, "did you expect?"

"So, WE'RE AGREED THEN, RIGHT?"

They were sitting face-to-face on pillows across a

low table in T.C.'s skylit loft. The blue early-morning sky filled the space like a canopy above them. T.C. had brewed fresh coffee and toasted thick slabs of corn bread, which he served with heavy, bittersweet marmalade.

"Agreed on what?" T.C. paused with the Mellior coffeepot still steaming in one hand.

"Agreed that last night should stand on its own merits until further notice, right?" She held up her blue mug and watched as he poured the coffee in a graceful arch from pot to cup. She was enjoying being waited on.

T.C.'s face was momentarily obscured by a cloud of steam. Then he put down the pot with a deliberate motion and looked at Tessa. "Is that what we've agreed on?"

"Well, you're going to San Francisco for that harbor reclamation project for six weeks, right?"

"Right. I leave tomorrow."

"That's right. And I . . . well, I've got to spend some time working. I haven't been putting in as much time as I should at the station."

"Really? It seems to me you work very hard there." He sipped his coffee and watched her over the top of his cup.

She wished he would not watch her so much. This was hard enough, trying to get things straight and settled, without going into nasty details. T.C. had mentioned his trip to the West Coast last night, and Tessa had seized on this news to remark that she, too, would be very busy in the next few weeks. He had said that that wasn't why he told her about the trip, but last night they had let it go at that. They had had other things to concentrate on.

This morning she wanted to make sure he understood. But she didn't want to tell him about Douglas. "I do work hard, but actually, I haven't been putting in much overtime, and the station sort of expects a certain amount." This much was true. She was never available on weekends when Tim McNulty, the Focus Team producer, wanted her. Either she had been in Baltimore or Douglas had been in Boston and unwilling to spend his time there alone.

"You're required to do overtime?" The question was put mildly, but Tessa knew T.C. was calling her bluff. You didn't spend a marvelous night with a man and then tell him you couldn't see him again because of overtime.

She sighed. "Actually, T.C., I've got to spend some time putting my life in order. You know, what I said about my past last night?"

"No." His response was prompt and somewhat tart. Was he upset, she wondered. Or just irritated? "I *don't* know, Tessa. I don't know what last night has to do with the rest of your life—especially with your past. The past is done with, and the future isn't here yet. What could that possibly have to do with last night?"

Tessa was unable to come up with a response to his relentless logic. She was also a bit offended that he should show so little interest in the rest of her life. Was that what it meant to have a one-night stand? That you totally ignored the rest of a person's life? Or was that just one of T.C.'s idiosyncrasies?

And she felt that T.C. was making it seem as if she *wanted* a further commitment, when that was the last thing she wanted at this point. She was only trying to be polite, she thought. Why was he so determined to ignore her hints about her involvement with another man? She wasn't sure which side of the argument she was on—or if there was an argument going on in the first place. It was all very frustrating.

She looked up at T.C. again. He had resumed eating, and didn't look as though he was involved in any argument. For a moment she envied him his ability to detach, to accept things as they were. But certain things had to be cleared up—even if this was to be a one-night stand. Besides, Tessa reminded herself, she wanted to be sure he didn't expect anything from her in the way of commitment. He certainly wasn't acting as though he did, but you never could tell.

She decided to try another tack. "Look. You're going away, right?"

"Right."

"And I'm . . . well, let's just say I'll be busy too, right?"

"Right. Want another piece of toast?" He held out a marmalade-slathered piece and she took it without pausing.

"Well then, all I'm saying is we won't be able to see each other for a while. That'll give us time to think."

"Think about what?" T.C. put down his toast. "Tessa, you are an incredible person to spend time with. Do you always use so much energy to dissect the world around you?"

He seemed genuinely curious. Tessa smiled wryly

and looked at his plate. The blue stoneware plate held a piece of toast that had been carefully bitten at all four corners, forming a lotus pattern of bread and jam. His knife was laid at a perfect right angle to the bread and was exactly perpendicular to the handle of his coffee cup. His napkin was folded in a perfect triangle.

"Look at your plate," she instructed him. "You see how carefully you've arranged everything on it? It doesn't look like breakfast, it looks like a still life! Now, look over here at mine." They both looked at her plate and laughed. Her toast was torn in half, and marmalade dripped over the edges. Her knife had slipped off the plate and rested precariously against her coffee cup, smearing jam on the handle. Even as they watched, the knife clattered to the table in a marmalade splash.

"You see? Anyone could tell you were concerned with space and design. It shows in the way you live. Me, I couldn't care less about that. But I care a lot about words and what they mean." She paused, forgetting for a moment her own train of thought. T.C. was watching her patiently, chewing carefully on a piece of bread. Tessa smiled affectionately. "I'm a good reporter, T.C.—a damn good reporter, just like you're a terrific architect. And I live my life with words. We both do things our way."

T.C. nodded slowly, as if digesting her words along with the toast. "I see. It's important to you to place last night in its proper perspective then, is that it? To figure out what it means in terms of the bigger picture of your life?"

Tessa was silent. She couldn't tell if he was making subtle fun of her or if he was really trying to understand something that was not familiar to him. She tried to step outside of herself and see the situation from his point of view. Here was a woman who came into his life, spent a remarkable night of lovemaking and then, in the morning, announced that they could not see each other again until she got her life in shape. He either saw her as someone trying to wheedle her way out of a further commitment, or wheedle her way into one. Or someone who was slightly crazy, which might be true.

But T.C. wasn't thinking about commitments at all. He simply could not fathom Tessa's penchant for clarification. Wasn't it enough that they had shared last night? That they were both unable to see each other for a while due to prior engagements? Wouldn't it be nice to spend this hour enjoying each other's company? He had his own plans for "later"—dreams, really, not plans—but to discuss them now was pointless.

They sat across from each other in silence for several minutes, each trying to decipher the other's message. It was strange, thought Tessa, how little they really knew each other, when last night they had been inside the other's skin so completely. For a moment she could not recall what it was about T.C. that even vaguely resembled her. He sat across from her, smooth-skinned, tawny and handsome in a white terry robe—she wore a wine-colored one of his. Did they look alike, or had last night been simply a trick of the subconscious, played on her vulnerable mind at a vulnerable time?

Then he smiled and reached across the table to take her hand. "You're right, of course," he said. "I've got a nasty habit of avoiding issues until they slip out of my grasp." He squeezed her fingers. "I don't want that to happen to last night."

Tessa waited for him to go on. Was he going to tell her he wanted to see her again when he got back, that he was sorry he would be leaving town? Much as Tessa was determined to leave herself an avenue of escape, she wished he would. Even if she could not agree to a future meeting, she would have liked him to offer.

But it seemed he wasn't about to. Apparently, he was satisfied to let their relationship go the way it was. "I'll tell you what," he said at last. "I'll be back in town in the middle of May. Why don't you call me if you've got some free time? Who knows—maybe we can celebrate our birthdays together. Yours is in June, too, isn't it?"

He was leaving it up to her. For a brief moment Tessa considered telling T.C. that she could commit to meeting him as easily as the next person—that she didn't always have to leave herself a way out.

But she did not. People who took on one-night stands didn't make serious declarations in the morning. Clearly, that was the message T.C. was trying to put through her thick skull. *Just let it go, Tessa*, she reminded herself. *After all, you're the one who never wants to get involved. Just let it go.*

So she smiled at him and lifted his hand to her lips, planting a brief kiss on his palm before returning it to him. And they spent another hour or so together, talking casually about their plans, careful not to include the other person in them, and careful not to let their thoughts roam too near the quilt that lay abandoned in a heap by the cold wood stove.

As soon as she left his apartment, Tessa began to see that she had done the right thing. After all, who was to say that she would even want to see T.C. again once she settled down to deal with the problem of Douglas—or the lack of Douglas. As it stood now, they had shared a remarkable night of love together, and she knew she would never be able to think of her breakup with Douglas without smiling at the memory of Thomas Chimatsu. If she never saw him again, she would recall him fondly, and with a little jolt in the pit of her stomach at the memory of what they had done together. If she did see him, that would be nice too—but only if their busy lives permitted it. It was all very grown-up.

Tessa smiled to herself as she wandered slowly through Back Bay, across the Boston Common and past Copley Square to the South End. This was what impulsive flings were all about, she decided. Taking the most out of the moment and then letting it go on the April breeze.

5

IT WASN'T as if she didn't intend to deal with the problem of Douglas Bright. Indeed, she half expected to find him waiting outside her apartment when she got back from T.C.'s and even had an excuse all ready for him. She would tell him she had been so upset that she had stayed at Lucinda's house that night. A cowardly excuse, she knew, but she was in no mood to explain where she had really been the night before.

He wasn't there, though, and there wasn't even a message on her answering machine from him. There was a message from Lucinda, asking her to call back and "tell me all about it"—meaning, presumably, Thomas Chimatsu. Tessa grimaced. One thing she did not want to do was dissect last night's experience with Lucinda. There was a limit to how much introspection one could indulge in, and with Lucinda, confessions were always dangerous.

So she left her answering machine on to deflect the possibility that Lucinda might call again, and to buy herself some time in case Douglas did call. Then she went to the station, was assigned an interminably boring State House press conference that got bumped from the air at the last moment and was back home before the 11:00 P.M. news show. The last thing she thought before falling asleep that night was "T.C.'s flying to California right at this minute." She fell asleep with a smile on her face.

The next morning she spent at home in a strange state of limbo. She sat in her window seat and watched the birds that had finally come to the bell feeder. It was another gloriously warm day, and the street below her filled with joggers and students, with mothers wheeling strollers and businessmen with umbrellas. Tessa couldn't remember when she had wasted hours so efficiently.

Every night that week when she got home from work, she would lie in bed for hours, waiting for sleep and perhaps for some sort of sorrow over Douglas to overcome her. *Maybe next week*, she thought sleepily, *when I've nothing to do all weekend—maybe then I'll come to my senses and realize what I'm missing.*

But the next week she scarcely had a chance to think, let alone dread the approach of the weekend. Tim McNulty had assigned her to a story on a nuclear disarmament protest being held outside an air-force base in New Hampshire, and Tessa managed to get permission to camp out at protest headquarters. She sent back reports via remote videotape and scooped all the other stations when dozens of the protesters were arrested for trespassing on federal property. She got back to Boston late Sunday night without even realizing that the weekend had gone by. Douglas had not called. Nor had Thomas.

The next few weeks were more of the same. Tim was pleased with the work she was doing and glad to have another reporter at his disposal for weekend work. Tessa got two other good assignments and a chance to co-anchor the Saturday night newscast when the regular anchor called in sick. She began to realize that her career at Channel 8 might indeed have been limited by the fact that she was never available on weekends. Although she was not about to let Tim exploit her sudden availability, she sensed that the station executives were not unaware of her increased visibility. Visibility was everything on TV news, as Doug had so often told her.

She also had more social obligations than she could handle. She saw Lucinda for dinner and a movie several times, although she flatly refused to attend any more parties. Lucinda, after one or two pointed questions about T.C. and the continued absence of Douglas Bright, wisely refrained from pressing Tessa for information on either subject. Tessa, in keeping with her new policy of "don't deal with it unless it's absolutely urgent," did not offer anything, either.

She did go to one party with several Channel 8 crew members, but, arriving back at her apartment at 3:00 A.M. with a raging headache, she decided that the single life did not necessarily mean subjecting oneself to hours of loud music and smoke-filled rooms. She even went out on a date one Saturday with an old friend who had once been romantically interested in her and apparently still was. But, though it was nice to have the attention, she politely declined his offer to spend the night with him.

She did not miss Douglas. As the weeks went by

and Douglas did not contact her, she was beginning to realize that there couldn't have been much of a commitment on his part either. It made Tessa feel better about her own lack in that department. It also made her realize that she was angry at him—very angry—for the way he had handled the whole thing, and that if he did call she would probably tell him to get lost.

She also didn't miss T.C., and this came as a pleasant surprise. Of course, she had not planned to miss him. In fact, she had planned to put him totally out of her mind. But she did *think* of him frequently, and with pleasure, although not with yearning. It was like having a gift waiting for her, tucked away in some secret corner of her mind. She could return to it and savor the thought whenever she wanted. No one else had to know about it—not even T.C.

Which was why she was so unprepared when they met again.

ON THE FIRST FRIDAY IN JUNE Tessa got a summons to Tim McNulty's office. She had spent the afternoon in the editing room, trying to finish a piece on a local lottery winner. The newsroom was in chaos, as it always was before a broadcast, and it was hard enough to think, let alone get anything accomplished. Annoyed at the interruption Tessa flung down her box of videotapes and stalked into Tim's office. She found him poring over some old tapes on his videocassette recorder.

"Recognize this, Tess?" Tim wheeled his chair aside so that Tessa could get a better view of the screen. She leaned over his shoulder to peer at the images of a large body of water surrounded by tall sentinel pines.

"It looks like a pond or a lake. Am I supposed to recognize it?"

Tim smiled. "Not if you didn't grow up around here, you aren't." Tim was a lanky, middle-aged Irishman who was always making fun of the poor souls who were not, like himself, Boston born and bred. "That's Choate Reservoir. Out past Worcester, in Choate Hollow."

Tessa made a face for his benefit. "Choate Hollow. How quaint and Yankee. Why is their pond so important?"

Tim shook his head dolefully. "You Southerners are all alike. That is a reservoir, not a pond, my dear girl. And it is the source of the water you drink, which is why it is so important."

"My drinking water comes from that?" Tessa wrinkled her nose. "You'd think it would taste cleaner than it does."

"Very funny. It has to travel to Boston through forty miles of old pipeline—that's why it tastes so lousy. And not only are those pipes corroded beyond belief, they are also tremendously overtaxed by the burden of providing water for a city that is two hundred times bigger than the reservoir was supposed to serve."

"Hmph. You'd think they'd have thought of that when they built the thing."

"Well, not everyone has your superior grasp of the world, Tessa, old girl. And that brings me to the subject of this meeting."

"You want me to figure out a way to get more water out of that lake."

"Reservoir."

"That reservoir."

Tim pursed his lips. "You think you can?"

"Sure. Just dig a deeper hole." She got up. "Is that all you wanted to know, Tim dear? Because I've got some editing to do for the six o'clock...."

"Sit down." She sat down. "Fortunately for the city of Boston, someone slightly more qualified than you has come up with an answer to that question. Which brings us to your next assignment. I want you to go out to Choate and give us something on the opening of the new Choate Reservoir."

Tessa gaped. "You mean they really are going to dig a deeper hole?"

"Another hole. And it's already there. They just have to fill it. How do you think the water got into the first one?"

"Wasn't it just . . . there?" She turned and looked at the video screen, which Tim had frozen on one frame. The reservoir stretched to the horizon in an unbroken expanse of sun-speckled blue. Only the military uniformity of the pine trees ringing the shore hinted at a less-than-natural scene.

"Ah, you city girls. . . . Do you think Mother Nature plants trees in concentric rings? Or digs perfect ovals for water?" Tim saw her perplexed expression and grinned. "Buck up, Miss Drew. That's why I'm sending you to the city water commission's planning meeting in—" he consulted his watch "—thirty minutes. The chief engineer will give you all the background you need. I'm sending you out on a seven-day field assignment starting next week. So pay attention and do your homework."

"Next week! But Tim, I've got two stories slated for next week. Good ones! And I've still got to get the voice-over on the six-o'clock."

"Let Arnie Case do the voice-over. You can do the Monday assignment next week, and I'll reassign the Wednesday story. That's the adoption agency, right?"

"But I wanted to do the adoption story!"

"Why? You planning to adopt?"

"Tim, be reasonable. What do I know about environmental affairs?"

He scowled. "Obviously very little."

"Right. So why don't you send someone else? Send Arnie. Send Elise, or Carl. Send anyone!" Tessa was not sure why she reacted so violently to the idea of going out in the field. She had been out many times before, and the fact that this one might take more than the usual day or two to shoot shouldn't have made any difference. But she was getting accustomed to the routine of work and home every day. She didn't like the idea of a break in her schedule.

Tim looked at his watch again. "You now have twenty-three minutes. The corner of State Street and Bowdoin. Take a cab."

"Tim, why me?"

"Because it's got some good human interest angles, I think, and you do good human interest stuff. Because you're up for a big field assignment, since you haven't done one in—oh, three years, I'd say." He paused to let this sink in. "Because you don't know the difference between a lake and a pond. Now go."

She went. And it was there, in the downtown office of the Metropolitan Water Commission that she found Thomas Chimatsu, looking for all the world as if he expected her.

He was sitting at the head of a long oval table in front of an easel, which held a series of architectural sketches. Around him sat several city officials and a number of other media people, most of whom Tessa recognized. But it was clear that Thomas Chimatsu was in charge here, and Tessa could only stare at him, flustered to the point of panic, while he sat there smiling affably at her.

"Ah," he said, rising and bowing cordially from the waist. "Our honored representative from WBOS—a bit late, but never mind. Now that everyone is here, I believe we can begin." He paused, waiting perhaps for Tessa to apologize for her tardiness, but Tessa neither moved nor spoke. "Won't you have a seat, Miss Drew?" T.C. offered politely.

Unfortunately, the only available seat was at the front, near him. Tessa began to wend her way through the silent room, excusing herself when someone had to move to let her by. She smiled weakly at several acquaintances, and several people greeted her by name, but mostly the room sat waiting in an awkward silence.

It wasn't until she had reached T.C. that the silence was broken. "Wait for me afterward," he whispered as she passed him. "We have some celebrating to do."

"Celebrating what?" She was too taken aback to whisper.

He smiled. "Your birthday, of course." Then he winked and turned to the rest of the group to begin the session.

It wasn't her birthday yet—that was still weeks away. And Tessa had never been told the exact date of T.C.'s birthday, even though she knew that, as a Gemini, it had to fall between May 21 and June 21. But the amazing thing was that she had forgotten completely about it. If T.C. hadn't reappeared in her life, and things had gone on at the same hectic pace, her birthday could easily have come and gone without her noticing.

Well, she probably would have gotten some cards in the mail, and a phone call from her parents in Virginia, where they had moved when Tessa left for college. And Lucinda or someone at the station might have remembered and organized some embarrassing scene or other to celebrate. But otherwise, for the first time in her life, Tessa had forgotten that she was turning a year older. The days and weeks had been flowing together so seamlessly that she scarcely paid attention to the passage of time.

Tessa now turned her attention to the matters at hand. It had finally begun to sink in that Thomas Chimatsu was more than just involved in the Choate Reservoir project—he was running the show. The Metropolitan Water Commission had hired his firm to manage the entire construction, from the design of the reservoir and pipelines to their execution, as well as the environmental landscaping the project would

entail. As chief engineer, with his extensive experience in aquatic engineering and environmental
landscaping, T.C. was a natural for the job.

She had to listen carefully to what he was saying in
order to fill in the huge gaps in her knowledge of the
project. T.C. gestured toward the easel, and Tessa
watched his graceful hands execute circles and para-
bolas on the paper, trying to concentrate on what he
said rather than on what he did. But she could not
help the warmth that grew up from her loins through
her ribs and to her cheeks at the thought of what
those hands had once done to her.

"The pipeline to the city is almost completed,"
T.C. was saying. "All we have to do now is to create
a flow-regulation mechanism between Choate I,
which is here, and Choate II, which will be here. As
you can see, the land forms a natural bowl, so we
don't have too much dredging left to do to complete
the excavation for Choate II. Once the last few ex-
isting properties on the land have been razed we'll be
able to go ahead and finish the work that nature
started for us. We should be ready to go by the end of
August."

A bell went off in Tessa's brain and she raised her
hand before she realized what she was doing. She remembered something she had read or heard about,
almost in passing, a long time ago. She saw T.C.'s
head swivel expectantly in her direction and she
fought to recall the details as quickly as possible.

"Miss Drew. Do you have a question?"

"Yes. I seem to recall—I'm not sure where I first
heard it, but back when Choate I was filled in,

weren't there some people who tried to stop it? They lost their homes, or something, and there was some question of whether the state had a right to—"

"Of course the state has a right!" This remark came from one of the state environmental officials, who scowled at Tessa. "Haven't you ever heard of eminent domain?"

Everybody's interest perked up, and Tessa saw some of the reporters scribbling furiously in their notebooks. She was still trying to recall where she had gleaned this little tidbit of information. When Tim had mentioned the Choate Reservoir the name had been vaguely familiar, but not until that moment had she connected it with the half-forgotten story.

"Adam, please sit down." T.C.'s tone was conciliatory but commanding. "As a matter of fact," he went on, turning to the group, "Miss Drew is right. When the first Choate Reservoir was built fifty years ago, it was necessary to relocate some nine hundred families who lived in the area. As a matter of fact, four townships were disbanded by state mandate, and there was some controversy over the matter.

"But when the last family was evacuated and the valley finally flooded, the arguments died down. After all, it was clearly a matter of the needs of the few being sacrificed for the needs of the many. And it's unlikely that the same scenario would happen today. There are only a few houses left on the land we'll be flooding, and the owners are willing to accept the generous relocation terms offered by the state. It appears—" he finished with a smile "—to have worked out well all around." He fixed the smile on Tessa, and it seemed to grow in intensity. "Have I explained myself clearly, Miss Drew?"

Tessa returned the smile. She was beginning to understand that covering this story could have its exciting moments—not the least of which would be questioning the chief engineer closely and at length. "I think you've told me enough for now," she said mildly. "Oh, but I do have one more question. Since there will be no more Choate Hollow once the second reservoir is completed, what does the state plan to label the project? Are we to refer to them as Choate I and Choate II?"

T.C. ducked his head for a moment and Tessa got the impression that he was chuckling under his breath. Once again, she got the feeling that he had anticipated her question. "As a matter of fact," he said, "I've been giving the matter some thought. Although I suspect the legal name will continue to be Choate Reservoir, I prefer to think of them as twin lakes, and to call them after my favorite astrological sign." He trained his gaze on Tessa, and she felt as if they were all alone in the room. "I would like to call them the Gemini Lakes."

6

"OF COURSE I SET IT UP," T.C. was saying to her. "I had to figure out a way to see you." He smiled and made the statement seem like the simplest one in the world to make.

"But how? How did you arrange it?" Tessa was, as usual, unwilling to accept such off-hand explanations. The reporter in her wanted to know more. "How did you know Channel 8 would assign me?"

"McNulty didn't spill the beans, then, huh?" T.C. grinned. "I specifically requested you for the piece. Told him I thought it suited your style of reporting, or some such line." He raised his hand as Tessa opened her mouth to object. "No, no, I don't mean that it isn't true. It *is* true, of course." He moved his hand forward and placed it squarely alongside her cheek. "It's really good to see you again," he said softly.

It *was* simple. Just like that. Tessa relaxed and chuckled. "Tim McNulty must have lapped it up. Especially the part about not letting me in on the plot. He loves plots."

"I'd rather call it a happy surprise than a plot," T.C. pointed out. "But McNulty owed me a favor from another project I had worked on a long time

ago. I gave him an exclusive once." He looked at her
and shook his head. "If you could have seen the look
on your face when you walked into that room!"

"Oh, I'll bet it was priceless." Tessa feigned pique.
She knew exactly how she must have looked. And
she wondered whether T.C. had been totally pleased
with his little "happy surprise." After all, she had
opened her mouth a number of times when he might
have preferred otherwise. "Anyway, I think you owe
me another beer. At least."

"At least." T.C. raised his hand to order a second
round. They were sitting in a tiny booth in a dark
and crowded pub near the Metropolitan Water Commission's offices. It was five-thirty on a Friday afternoon, and the city's employees were hanging about
longer than usual before subjecting themselves to the
ordeal of rush-hour traffic. The level of noise in the
room was high, but they had managed to find a corner table far from the jukebox and the jovial commotion at the copper bar. "Don't forget, we've come to
celebrate an occasion of note. To the Gemini Lakes."

Tessa raised her glass against his. "To the Gemini
Lakes."

"To the Gemini Lakes," T.C. repeated. "I just hope
it's not premature. A lot of things can happen between now and September."

"Such as what?" Tessa watched T.C. stare ab-
stractedly into his glass. His fingers traveled up and
down the barrel-shaped sides, leaving runny rivers in
the frost. She wondered why he hadn't made a toast
to their birthdays as well, but decided not to mention
it. "What could possibly go wrong?" she repeated.

He glanced up. "Are you asking as Tessa Drew, Focus Team reporter?" he asked warily.

She grinned. "I'm asking as Tessa Drew, insatiable questioner. I'm just curious, that's all."

He reached across the table and took her hand. His was cool and damp from the glass, and she covered it with her other hand. It seemed very natural to be affectionate with T.C., even though they had yet to reestablish any intimate contact, or even discuss whether they planned to. It just happened that they were holding hands.

"I remember," he said quietly, and she knew he was not just remembering her passion for words and answers. They looked at each other for a moment in silence, then he went on. "But I'll tell you, Tessa, I really don't know what could happen. Anything from some politician throwing a wrench in the works to an unusual dry spell, which will make all of us look like damn fools." He shrugged. "It's the luck of the draw, as always."

"Don't you hate that? Being made to look like a fool when it's out of your control?"

"No. I know I've done what had to be done. If the Gemini Lakes never become a reality, then they don't. My part in it will be finished by then in any case." He smiled and changed the subject smoothly. "But you must admit, the idea of calling it the Gemini Lakes was a brainstorm."

"A stroke of genius." Tessa wondered if she should mention that she had thought of him often in these past six weeks. Not that she had missed him, because that would be overstating the case, but just to let him know that she had occasionally thought of him and smiled. No, better not make a statement like that, she decided. After all, he had not mentioned missing her so it was better not to bring up the subject at all. "How was San Francisco?" she asked instead.

"Cold and rainy," he replied. "I spent most of my time sloshing about in puddles under the old Fisherman's Wharf. But I saw some relatives there that I haven't seen for years, and that was nice."

"What relatives?" She reached out idly and began nibbling popcorn from the bowl the waitress had placed on their table. "Don't eat that," he admonished gently. "We're going to dinner to celebrate, aren't we?"

"Tell me about your relatives," she repeated, taking her fingers out of the popcorn bowl.

He grinned at her persistence. "My father's uncle," he said. "He's eighty-six and still working, making rice-paper scrolls to sell to tourists in Chinatown. I hadn't seen him since I was six years old."

"What did he think of you?" Tessa asked.

T.C. paused reflectively and answered in a solemn voice, as if she had asked an important question. "He thinks I've become what I should have become," he said. His eyes were fixed on some faraway point, and Tessa had a sudden image, not necessarily accurate but very clear, of a tiny wizened man bent over a low table with an ink quill poised between bony fingers.

"What does that mean?" She was not sure if he even heard her, but T.C. blinked and then looked at her, his eyes once again clear and smiling.

"It means," he told her, "that the old man didn't

know what to make of me, and knew he could get away with it by sounding cryptic."

Tessa grinned. "Very Japanese," she said. It was becoming their private joke. Both of them knew that appearances were often deceiving. And it was nice to share a private joke—like sharing a history.

"Very." T.C. finished his beer in one swig and set the mug firmly down on the table. "So. Where shall we go for dinner? You're the birthday girl."

"You're the birthday boy," she countered.

"That is true. So I vote for somewhere that has great birthday cake."

Tessa laughed. "A restaurant that serves birthday cake?"

"Sure. All you have to do is tip off the waiter that it's to be a big surprise. They love to come out of the kitchen singing with a candle stuck in the pie à la mode, even at the poshest joints."

"I don't believe you." Tessa giggled.

"You don't? Well, then, Miss Curiosity, I suggest we go to the poshest of the posh and check it out."

THEY WENT TO THE RITZ.

First they stopped at Brooks Brothers across the street from the venerable Boston hotel, where T.C. bought a navy-blue tie with a red fleur-de-lis pattern. Ignoring the salesman's obvious dismay, he knotted it carefully around his turtleneck while Tessa stood by, inspecting the results. Then she handed him his sports jacket and they stood together arm in arm in front of the mahogany-trimmed triple mirrors in the store, smiling at the six identical figures who gazed

back at them—a veritable crowd of look-alikes in
their coincidental outfits of navy-blue and tan.

Since it was still early, they managed to find a corner table in the Ritz dining room without reserva-
tions. The room was starched and quiet, gleaming
with heavy napery and silver and the famous air of
hushed luxury. The waiters were all swift and
solemn, and the other diners were all senior citizens
at this unfashionable hour. T.C. and Tessa sat down,
and Tessa demurely busied herself with the menu
while T.C. took the maître d' aside for a hushed conference.

The meal itself was superb. They started off with
pale croquettes of scallop in delicate salmon sauce,
and then a salad of lacy Boston lettuce and *radicchio*
in a light raspberry-vinegar dressing. Tessa had
swordfish broiled to perfection, and T.C. ordered
beef tournedos that came with a heady Madeira
gravy.

There was a pregnant pause between the main
course and dessert. Tessa and T.C. dared not meet
each other's eyes for fear of bursting into laughter,
which would have ruined the ritualistic mood of the
dining room. All they could hear was the muted clink
of silver and the low hum of cultured conversation.
Would the Ritz kitchen honor T.C.'s request? Tessa
could not imagine the poker-faced waiters bursting
into song.

But they did. There was a short commotion near
the kitchen, and then they began. Four waiters, led
by the maître d', advanced on their table, smiling as
they sang "Happy Birthday" to Tessa. And to Tessa's

amazement, almost everyone in the dining room turned around and joined in. It was as if the entire event had been choreographed and the diners were just waiting for the cue to break out of their staid molds and into the hilarity of the occasion.

With a flourish, the maître d' presented Tessa with her dessert. It was not pie à la mode, but a small baked Alaska, the snowy meringue tipped with brown and crowned with a slender sparkler that sputtered and glowed in a shower of sparks. Tessa looked at T.C., who was watching with fond amusement. She tried to say something witty, but found her throat curiously clutched. What had begun as a joke had turned into a very special experience for her. The roomful of smiling, nodding strangers, the ridiculous opulence of the baked Alaska on its china serving plate and, most of all, T.C.'s smile across the table—she had not expected it to mean so much.

"Miss Drew," said the maître d', "we watch you on television whenever we can. Happy birthday, and we're glad you decided to celebrate with us at the Ritz."

"So am I," she managed to say. "So am I." Then, when the waiters had backed away and they were left alone, she said, "But it's your birthday too, T.C. I want this to be special for you, too." She wondered if he caught the tremble in her voice.

"It is special for me," he said, laying his hand over hers. "And besides, if you think I'm going to let you eat that whole thing, you're crazy!"

Even for two self-avowed sweet tooths, the dessert was too much for them to handle. They finished up with strong coffee and brandy, and Tessa began to feel the spreading glow of satiation in addition to the pleasure she took in T.C.'s company.

T.C. allowed her to make token attempts at splitting the bill, which was exorbitant, and then insisted that it was his birthday gift to her.

"But it isn't even my birthday yet," she argued. "And I probably missed yours altogether. You never *did* tell me the date. I want to do something to celebrate."

T.C. stood up behind her to help pull out her chair. As she stood, he leaned over and spoke softly against her hair. "I was hoping we could celebrate in bed," he said.

No one else in the room could possibly have heard him. But the effect of his quiet statement was so explosive for Tessa that she felt as if everyone in the room must be frozen with horror. She bit her lip and looked around guiltily, and actually stumbled against the table so that the china rattled.

"Don't you think," whispered T.C. without a trace of a grin, "that you could be a little more discreet?"

Tessa regained her composure and turned to face him. He looked self-contained and serious, standing there with that preppy tie knotted so neatly and ludicrously around his turtleneck. It was hard to believe that this elegant man had just whispered so outrageously in her ear. Tessa grinned at him. Two could play at this game, she thought.

"Sure—" she grinned, making certain her voice carried through the room "—your place or mine?"

THEY ENDED UP AT HER PLACE. Tessa was glad she had done some spring cleaning, so the place was at least minimally acceptable for sudden visitors. But, unlocking the door to her third floor walk-up and switching on the lights in her canary-yellow living room, it seemed that she was seeing everything through T.C.'s expert eye—and all she could see was clutter.

T.C., however, was impressed. "This looks exactly like you," he said delightedly as he roamed around the small room with its semicircular bay window overlooking the street. "It's so warm and full of curiosity!"

"It's curious, all right." Tessa dashed over to the brick fireplace, which was full of old papers she had been meaning to burn for weeks. From where she stood she could see into the kitchen, where her breakfast glass of high-protein milk shake still stood, unwashed, on the butcher-block counter near the sink. A faint acrid smell told her she had forgotten to turn off the electric coffee maker again this morning. She grimaced.

"That's okay," T.C. said, seeming to read her mind. He sat down on the couch and put his legs up on the antique trunk she used as a coffee table. "It uses a ridiculous amount of electricity but it doesn't ruin the coffee maker."

"Sure does ruin the coffee, though," she said glumly, plopping herself down next to him. She looked around at the room. "I really need to unclutter my life," she announced.

"That's what you said six weeks ago," he said.

She looked at him, stunned. "Yes," she replied slowly, "I think I did mention something about that."

"Well, did you unclutter your life at all?"

She shook her head. She was astounded that he should be asking, just when she had convinced herself that the subject had never crossed his mind. "What do you think?" she asked. "Just take a look around. Ye olde curiosity shoppe, that's what I live in."

T.C. let his gaze travel slowly around the room, while his arms reached out to pull her closer to him on the couch. "I have taken a look around," he pronounced carefully after a pause. "And, if you ask me—" he lowered his lips to hers as he spoke "—there's a lot less here than meets the eye." He lifted his hand and placed it firmly against her breast. "And a lot more *here*."

"I guess I'm supposed to ask you what that means," Tessa murmured against his neck. She was suddenly feeling both exhausted and aroused and wanted only to lie naked in his loving embrace. "But you don't mind if we act now and talk about what it means later, do you?"

He used the hand that was over her breast to begin unbuttoning the top of her shirtwaist, slipping the other arm along the back of her neck so he could lower her onto the couch beneath him. "That," he said between tiny, biting kisses, "is a very Oriental thing to say."

They both laughed and then stopped talking in order to concentrate on what was happening with their bodies. Based on what had happened last time,

Tessa knew to relax her body completely and wait for it to tell her what to do next rather than to follow any prescribed rules of foreplay. It took more time that way, but the time it took to reach ultimate fulfillment was exquisitely spent. They lay for a moment side by side on the couch then shifted so they could remove the rest of their clothing. Then, they lay back down and concentrated on letting their bodies come together at as many points of contact as possible.

T.C. used his mouth in ways Tessa had never imagined. Not only his lips, but his tongue and his teeth and his chin came into play—reaching, exploring and bestowing gifts on Tessa's face, neck and breasts. She was becoming lost in him—in his mouth, his neck, the narrow crevice behind his ear—finally resting her mouth on the pillowy expanse that the surface of his skin had become. There were feathery kisses, moist, lingering kisses and deep, hungry ones that betrayed their bodies' anxiety to move on.

Then the kisses were no longer enough and, despite her efforts to relax and maintain control over the ebb and flow of her desire, Tessa found herself vibrating with the need to do more, to explore further. T.C.'s body was warm to the touch, and she could not keep her fingers, her lips, from grasping for more of that faintly sandalwood-scented flesh. They shifted on the couch so that she lay back against the loose chintz cushions and he knelt on the tiny Oriental rug before her. Her thighs wrapped around the velvet-cloaked musculature of his torso, and she ran her legs up and down his flanks, sighing at the luxury of the sensation of steel beneath silk. Then, lifting himself over

her on one knee, he entered her just at the most poig-
nant moment, and nothing else existed except the
sensation with which he filled her and the ecstasy
they reached together.

THEY MOVED INTO HER BEDROOM at some point and lay
beneath the old patchwork quilt just staring at each
other for a long time before they started to make love
again. And they continued to make love for much of
the night, until Tessa felt she had lost the ability to
distinguish between his body and her own. It was all
pleasure, eagerly sought and gently shared, and
nothing else existed but themselves.

It was near dawn when Tessa realized that she could
not move another muscle, regardless of the pleasure
that motion would inevitably cause. She thought T.C.
was still deep inside her, but when she looked to the
side, she saw that he was not. He smiled and kissed the
tip of her nose. "We have to rest now," he said tenderly, and he reached up to stroke the damp tendrils of
hair that curled around her forehead.

Tessa nodded, cocked her ear to listen to something and then smiled sleepily. "Hear that? That's the
birds outside my window. I feed them and they come
back every year."

T.C. turned his head and looked over to the small
bay window that looked out onto the treetops in the
back of Tessa's building. "I hear," he said, turning
back to her. "Wood sparrows, aren't they? Or maybe
robins. It's a beautiful sound."

"I missed you, T.C." It was little more than a
sleepy murmur, but he heard.

"Shhh," he whispered, stroking her forehead in a hypnotic rhythm. "I know, I know. Now go to sleep."

She already had. So she did not hear him offer the last toast of the evening. "To the Gemini Lakes. To us. And to you, Tessa, to you."

7

THE SLEEPY HOLLOW MOTEL was nestled in a small valley just outside the village of Choate Hollow. Tessa arrived there with her cameraman, Paul Manning, a week later, only to find that the motel manager had no record of her reservation. Paul, who wasn't looking forward to his hundred-mile commute back and forth to Boston, was all for giving up and going right home. But Tessa was able to persuade the manager that she deserved a room, and that her employers would be good for the bill. She had her own reasons for being persuasive, and she was even able to take some good-natured ribbing from Paul about being cooped up in a one-horse town for two weeks without even a movie theater to liven up her nights. She had considered other possibilities for the evenings.

"Do you know how big this town is?" Paul had inquired as he helped her unload her belongings into the small room she was assigned. "Or rather, how small?"

Tessa grinned. "How small is it, Paul?"

"I just read the sign on the post office door. Actually, it's the general store door, but it's the post office, too. And the gas station. It said, Choate Hollow,

Population 36, U.S. Post Office, Greyhound Bus
Terminal, Bank of New England, Choate Hollow
Branch. Please Honk for Gas. Please honk for gas.
Do you believe that?''

Tessa had to laugh at his expression of wonder and
scorn. ''Come on, Paul, what's it to you? You can get
back to the city every night if you feel so nervous out
here in the wilds of central Massachusetts. Besides, I
would think you'd enjoy shooting out here more than
you would taking shots of tenement fires in Dor-
chester.''

Paul appeared to be debating it seriously for a moment, then shook his head. ''Population 36. I wonder
if that's before or after the reservoir workers came in.''

Grinning, Tessa chased him out of the room and
pulled out her typewriter and tape recorder before
opening her suitcase and rummaging through it for a
change of clothes. She wasn't sure when she would
run into T.C.—he might even be staying at the
motel—but she wanted to look her best when she did
see him.

Tessa changed into a pair of lemon-yellow chinos
and a royal-blue blouse of Egyptian cotton with pale-
yellow stripes. She brushed her hair until it shone
and then, notebook in hand, went out into the strong
June sun. Early summer blazed forth with a vengeance out there in the hills, and everything looked
freshly made in the clear morning light. Tessa and
Paul discussed their strategy for pictures and text and
went to the local diner for lunch. Then Paul left for
Boston, since they were not planning to go up to the
construction site for photos until the following day.

Tessa remained in her room all afternoon organizing her strategy, reading background material and making phone calls for interviews. But all the while in the back of her mind was the question, *When will I see T.C.?*

They had not made specific plans to meet. All he had told her, when he left her apartment the morning after their birthday celebration, was that he might be staying in the area and that he would surely be able to find her if she couldn't find him.

"This is a hard-hat job," he had told her, kissing the tip of her nose in a way that made her feel tiny and delicate even though they were almost the same height. "And believe me, when a woman appears on a hard-hat site—especially a woman like you—the ripples are visible for miles. I'll know you're there."

Tessa had interpreted this as an unspoken request not to appear on the site until she had been invited, and she bristled. "You should be reported to the feminist police for a remark like that," she chided.

He shrugged. "I didn't say I did the gawking. I'm just saying that's the way it is. Some things don't change until they're ready to change. You know that."

Tessa wasn't sure she did. "Then people should work to make them change faster," she retorted.

He gathered her against his chest for a final caress. "Now listen, when you get out to Choate Hollow, just call and set up an appointment with Commissioner Conklin. He'll bring you out to the site. See you then."

And he had kissed her and left it at that. At the

time, still full of the sight and smell and feel of him, she had not bothered to worry about it. But now, as the afternoon waned into night, her eager anticipation had begun to evaporate into loneliness. Paul was right. Who wanted to spend weeks out here in the middle of nowhere, covering a story that would probably amount to nothing, without a little companionship to wile away the hours?

Well, it was clear that T.C. was not staying at the Sleepy Hollow Motel, so Tessa finished her work, had a solitary dinner in the motel dining room and fell asleep early, dreaming of warm, graceful hands and sunlit bowls of blue water under the summer sky.

She awoke feeling considerably more expectant and excited. After all, she was bound to see T.C. sooner or later, and the anticipation was part of the pleasure. She had set up her first interview for that morning, and getting down to work on a story always made her feel terrific. She was as eager to get to work on the Gemini Lakes story as she was to see T.C.—well, almost.

Her first interview was with Dan McGregor, one of the farmers who had sold his home to the state. As a matter of fact, his home had already been razed, so they met for the interview at the home of his sister-in-law.

"Yes, this is the best thing to happen to the valley since Choate I," McGregor told her. "Why, those fellows from the water commission gave me more for my farm than I could ever have hoped to get on the open market." He grinned unevenly at Tessa and gestured with tobacco-stained fingers. "Not that it was much of a farm left to sell. But if you ask me, I got the better end of the deal!"

He was colorful, Tessa decided, but only marginally so. She asked him to arrange a time when she could come back and interview his sister-in-law, who lived in the large white house by herself. But he had merely grinned again and told her she would have to arrange that herself.

By 3:00 P.M. she was on the site to interview the state water commissioner, Tom Conklin. Despite Tessa's professional skill, she had to make an effort to concentrate on what he was saying. First of all, the place was beautiful. The photos she had been studying had not done it justice. The deep bowl of the reservoir glistened like an elongated blue opal, separated from the cloudless sky by the neat green garland of trees. So far, the only signs of heavy construction were confined to one corner of the ridge, so that one could stand facing in the other direction and imagine the lake as a serene natural hideaway—a gift from Mother Nature to the world.

But the action on the ridge was impossible to ignore, since the loud hectoring of the jackhammers filled the still air, and Tessa was well aware that somewhere among the various knots of hard-hatted workers was Thomas Chimatsu.

T.C. had been right about one thing, she realized. Her passage, as she hurried along beside the water commissioner so her portable tape mike could pick up what he was saying, created a noticeable wave of interest.

She almost didn't need to have her recorder trained on the commissioner's every word. What he said was so predictable that she could have written it herself. But, aside from journalistic integrity, she was grateful for the distraction it afforded, for the first person she saw when they approached the trailer being used as site headquarters was T.C. himself.

He was standing on the top step of the trailer, and had just tipped his yellow hat back so that the sun flowed fully across his finely sculpted features. Tessa concentrated on watching the commissioner and keeping the mike positioned in front of his mouth, but she could not control the anticipatory tremble in her hand, nor the delicious drop in the pit of her stomach at the sight.

He saw her, too, and paused on the top step to watch her approach. A slow smile crept across his features, and by the time Tessa and the commissioner had reached the trailer his expression was warm and amused.

"Good afternoon, Tom," he said to the commissioner, and before Tom could begin the proper introductions he came down the steps toward Tessa. "And welcome to the Gemini Lakes, Miss Drew," he said, extending his hand cordially. "Glad you could make it." His handshake was warm, but without any secret messages in the grip.

"I've been here since yesterday," she said, wondering why she said it.

"Oh, really? I could tell you were coming from all the way down the ridge," he told her, and she got a flash of that secret smile. "But the hard-hat hotline doesn't extend to the hollow, I guess. You must be staying at the motel in Choate, with the other reporters."

"There aren't many other reporters, but yes, that's where I am." Tessa wondered if they were really conducting this conversation on as many levels as she thought they were and, if they were, whether the commissioner noticed.

"Well, if anything exciting happens, you'll be the first one with the news," T.C. said. Then he turned to the commissioner and began to discuss a technical matter, clearly intending for Tessa to stand by quietly and listen.

She wasn't sure how to take it. On the one hand, she felt he had clearly been trying to find out where she was staying, which could only mean that he planned to get in touch with her later on. On the other hand, his ability to act as if there was nothing out of the ordinary between them was disconcerting. She could not read him well enough to tell how he expected her to respond.

She tried to pick up on what they were saying. Mr. Conklin was muttering something about an old lady, his thick features compressed into a frown of disapproval.

"What's this about an old lady?" Tessa inquired, making sure that her microphone switch was on, even though she now held the mike at a discreet distance from the speakers. She was enough of a realist to know when to keep her reportorial self at a low profile and enough of a professional to know that as long as she hadn't been told the material was off the record she should get it on tape.

Commissioner Conklin looked at her as if he had completely forgotten her presence. "Oh, nothing, nothing, don't worry about it," he said paternally.

T.C. smiled. "I don't think Miss Drew was worried," he said gently, "I think she was curious." Conklin gave him an odd look, but T.C. went on, turning to Tessa politely. "Tom is telling me that we're having a bit of trouble with one of the homeowners whose home is slated for demolition next week. A Miss McGregor, I believe."

"Is that Dan's sister-in-law? I just met with him in her house." Tessa recalled the funny smile Dan McGregor had given her when she asked him to help her arrange an interview with his sister. Her reporter's heart beat a notch faster.

"Yes, that's Beryl," said Tom quickly. "But you don't have to.... I wouldn't bother getting interested, Miss Drew. Beryl's planning to come around, I know." He turned to T.C. and his voice became plaintive. "After all, we've scheduled the crew and everything."

T.C. was still smiling, but his eyes were opaque. "It might be interesting for Tessa to talk to her," he mused, almost to himself. "Might make an interesting story."

"I don't think it would be interesting," grumbled Tom.

"What's she like?" Tessa asked T.C., her eyes shining with anticipation and curiosity.

He watched her face for a moment before answering. "She's committed," he said briefly, and then they were interrupted by someone calling T.C. from inside the trailer.

"Would you excuse me for a moment?" he inquired politely, and disappeared up the steps into the trailer without waiting for a reply. Commissioner Conklin looked after him, shaking his head. "Hell of a guy," he muttered, "hell of a guy." Then, turning to Tessa, he spoke in a tone that was clearly intended to steer the conversation away from Beryl McGregor. "What do you think of a guy like that? You never really know what he's thinking, but he sure knows his stuff. He did that Elliott Sanctuary—know it?"

"I've heard of it," Tessa replied. She was drinking in every morsel of information she could find about Thomas Chimatsu.

"Those environmental activists," said Commissioner Conklin with a snort, "they all complained that he was ruining the natural environment. Hah! It never occurred to them that the natural environment had been so badly eroded that the wildlife was dying out by the score. Environmentalists. Hah!"

Sill harrumphing, he moved off down the ridge, and Tessa, after a swift glance back at the trailer, followed. Conklin was right—you never really did know what Thomas Chimatsu was thinking. What prompted his actions? What made him tick? Tessa had assumed that, because he was a Gemini and because he resembled her, he was like her. But she was beginning to see that he was not. His personal commitments, whatever they were, did not infringe on his professional commitments. He was a man who had the courage of his convictions, and she envied this quality in him, since she herself was never exactly sure what she was committed to. But to what else was T.C. committed? Or to whom? She remembered his remark on their first night together. ". . . my track record is not that great when it comes to certain commitments." Obviously he was referring to past relationships. At least, Tessa could only hope they were past.

But what about now? How did he feel about the Gemini Lakes, about people like the McGregors? They were hardly dying out in droves in their natural habitat, even though their numbers were dwindling. Could T.C. reconcile the loss of their homes the way he reconciled the Elliott Sanctuary?

She had no way of knowing, except to get to know him better, and she had every intention of doing just that. Whatever he was committed to, she saw no harm in his being committed to her—if only on a short-term basis. After all, that was all she wanted, wasn't it? There was nothing wrong with that, as long as both of them were aware that now was not the time for a long-term relationship. Tessa knew it, and she was sure T.C. did too.

Besides, she had a lot to learn from the guy, aside from the information he could offer her about the Gemini Lakes. She liked the way he handled his professional life, the way he was able to divorce his private self from his public self. That was a lesson Tessa knew she could benefit from learning. As a matter of fact, there were several lessons she could learn from T.C., and one of the best had to be taught in private.

The question was, when could she arrange for her next lesson?

CONSIDERING THE NATURE of her musings about T.C., it was amazing to Tessa that she did not spend more time thinking about ways to get to see him. But the next few days were so totally absorbed in following up on the Gemini Lakes story that she literally did not have a moment to think, much less scheme. And, as it turned out, her fears that the story might turn out to be a humdrum one became groundless on the very next day.

At first, she had not thought much about the interview she had set up with Dan's sister-in-law, Beryl McGregor. She was, Tessa imagined, simply an old woman who didn't want to let her house go. Beryl McGregor was probably a classic eccentric, Tessa decided, barely worth the tape it would take to record her.

But then she remembered Dan McGregor's funny smile, and the look on T.C.'s face when he had said it might be interesting for them to meet. And, when she finally got the old woman on the phone, she was even more intrigued.

"Ah," said Beryl McGregor with a deep chuckle when Tessa identified herself, "so you've finally decided to get in touch!" She sounded pleased.

Tessa, who had been expecting a curt refusal or a rude hang-up, was taken aback by the cordial humor in the woman's voice. She didn't sound like a crazy old lady. "You...were you expecting me?" she asked.

"In a manner of speaking...yes, you might say I was. Now...you know where I am, right? You were here with Dan."

"Yes," she began, "Mr. McGregor said it was. . . ." She stopped. But before she could continue, Beryl McGregor instructed, "You'll come here tomorrow at three. I serve tea—a big tea, so don't eat lunch. And please, don't bring your photographer this time. See you then."

And she rang off.

THE FOLLOWING AFTERNOON, Tessa dropped Paul at the site to do some extra background shooting and drove down the short dirt road that led to Beryl McGregor's farmhouse.

It was not really a farmhouse, since there was no farm surrounding it. But it did have the requisite white clapboards, albeit a little grayed with age, and the classic tall windows, with the kitchen off in an ell that extended out into an untidy garden in the back-yard.

The front door was open, and the screen hung loosely in its frame. Tessa, after looking unsuccessfully for a bell, called out for her hostess several times. There was no sound from the dim interior of the house except for the rhythmic swing of a clock. After a moment's pause, Tessa let herself in.

At first she thought that Beryl might have forgotten about the visit. But then she peered into the kitchen and saw the table laid neatly for two, with matching place mats, heavy pottery plates and teacups and even a delicate arrangement of baby's breath and day lilies in a stoneware vase.

It was not the sort of fussy table a forgetful old woman would lay. It looked more like a table that one of Tessa's contemporaries might set, artful yet minimal, with the accent on design rather than clutter.

Hoping that she could get a handle on this strange woman before the interview began, Tessa wandered back into the living room. The walls were lined with bookshelves stuffed with more than books. Fragments of an entire active life could be put together if one studied those dark wooden shelves. There were photos, knickknacks, piles of papers, even a group of newspaper clippings, now yellow and brittle with age. Tessa stepped closer and read the headline on the nearest clipping. "'Four area towns are slated for Reservoir Project,'" she read, and, under it, "'850 families will relocate, according to state officials.'" The date was June 17, 1935.

Tessa bit her lip. June 17 was her birthday, less than a week away. She didn't believe in coincidences, she reminded herself. Anyway, coincidences were just that—accidents of fate, and not talismans of the future. Take herself and T.C....

"History repeats itself, don't you think?"

Tessa swung around. Beryl McGregor was sitting on a small wing-backed armchair, looking as if she had been sitting there for hours.

"Miss McGregor! I'm sorry, I hope you don't think I was intruding, but I . . . ." Tessa let her hands fly expressively around the air in front of her, at a loss for words.

"I left the door open for you to come in. A person'd have to be pretty stubborn to ignore an invitation like that." There was no malice in her voice, but her blue eyes blazed steadily up at Tessa.

Tessa was silent. She had the uncomfortable feeling that Beryl knew more about her than she did about Beryl—not a particularly advantageous situation for a reporter to be in. The woman sitting before her was small, careworn but well constructed, like her house. Her hair was a nondescript blond-gray, and she wore her neat blue jeans and a blue work shirt as if they grew on her body. She sat like a neat little package on the chair, feet placed carefully together and hands folded demurely in her lap.

But there was nothing demure about her face, which was creased with wary intelligence. She was waiting patiently for Tessa to say something, and Tessa knew it. Beryl McGregor both unnerved and fascinated her, and she reminded her vaguely of someone she knew. But who?

"Miss McGregor, it was nice of you to let me come on such short notice." When in doubt, Tessa reminded herself, start with the basics. Once she got the ball rolling, the interview would develop a life of its own, as it always did.

"Thank you. It was no trouble at all. And please, call me Beryl—everyone does." She smiled gently and waited for Tessa to set up her tape recorder.

"Beryl. It's a nice name." This was said sincerely for, in spite of herself, Tessa was beginning to be genuinely intrigued by Beryl McGregor, always a sign that she would enjoy her interview and her subject.

"I was named after a semiprecious stone," Beryl said.

Tessa grinned. "It suits you. So does this house. How long have you lived here?"

Beryl smiled. "I was born here," she said softly,
and though there was no sadness in her voice, Tessa
got a sudden hint of the well of sorrow that the
woman must feel at the prospect of seeing her birth-
place sunk beneath thirty feet of water.

To avoid confronting the pain she knew must be in
those bright-blue eyes, Tessa looked down, pretending to be consulting her notes. Usually she did not
work from notes, preferring spontaneous conversation with her subjects to bring out the most revealing
information. She had a knack for getting people to
tell her what was on their minds. But today she was
thrown off her pace by the still, small woman who
sat before her. She felt that Beryl McGregor would be
glad to tell her exactly what was on her mind, once
she was asked.

And she wasn't disappointed. Beryl McGregor answered Tessa's questions honestly and articulately,
but without once overstepping the bounds of the
question. She talked about the history of the valley
and about her life in the house. She had been born in
it, moved away and had only returned after her
parents' death a dozen years ago. Beryl also spoke of
the possibility of moving in with a sister in Worcester
and of writing her memoirs, which she had been
planning to do for years.

She never once mentioned the fact that she was
planning to resist the demolition plans for her house
or the fact that her life would be buried beneath tons
of water when the Gemini Lakes finally became reality. But all through the interview, which lasted over
two hours, Tessa was increasingly aware of a sense of

leashed power, as if Beryl were forcibly holding herself back from talking about the things that really mattered.

They had tea, which was indeed a vast meal, and talked until nearly dark. Beryl walked Tessa to the car and even gave her a bunch of early lilacs to take back to her hotel room. She stood in the driveway waving until Tessa's car was out of sight.

But as soon as she left, Tessa's sense of discomfort grew into acute anxiety. She had botched the interview, that was all there was to it. Somehow that woman had managed to make Tessa uneasy about asking any questions. She felt both angry and defeated and unable to explain the impact the woman had had on her. And for some strange reason, she wanted to see T.C.

She didn't have long to wait. When she got back to her motel room there was a note pinned to her door. "Be back for you in an hour. Gone to find you a sleeping bag. T.C."

8

"DO YOU HAVE ANY IDEA how hard it is to find a sleeping bag around here?"

T.C. was leaning against the door to her motel room when she opened it. He looked suitably fatigued. "I've been to every hardware store, every dry-goods store, every grocery store in the area. No one even carries them."

Tessa made a wry face as she stepped aside to let him in. He was almost an hour later than she'd expected, and she hoped the irritation, and now relief, didn't show on her face. "That couldn't have taken very long," she said. "I didn't even know there were three stores of any description around these parts."

T.C. sighed. "Everybody looked at me like I was crazy. Why on earth would anyone want to sleep outside, they seemed to be asking me? Why not just move your bed near the window?" He shook his head.

Tessa grinned. "You must admit, they have a point. After all, these folks grew up in the great outdoors. Their idea of adventure is probably a night at the Boston Motor Inn."

"You're right. To each his own—or her own, as the case may be." He took her by the arm and led her back to the opened door. "Fortunately for us citified nature hounds, I did find a suitable sleeping bag—in Worcester."

"You *did* do some hunting!" Tessa peered at the low red sports car parked in front of her door. "How did you fit it in that toy car?"

T.C. pretended to be hurt. "What? You don't like my Fiat?"

She went out into the warm evening and ran her hands along the smooth low hood. It was exactly the kind of car she had always dreamed of owning— small, fast and a joy to handle. Tessa had a passion for nice cars, even though the only auto she had ever owned was a hand-me-down Karmann Ghia, which broke down when the temperature fell below fifty degrees.

She wouldn't have thought it was the kind of car Thomas Chimatsu would drive. But she had learned to expect the unexpected from him, and she could not deny that the idea pleased her no end. Now she leaned against the driver's door and grinned at him. "I love your Fiat," she said in what she hoped was a suitably sexy voice.

His smile told her it was. "I'm glad. Want to drive?" He held out a set of keys. Tessa's face lit up and she instinctively reached out for them. Then she paused.

"I'd adore driving it. But you haven't mentioned where we're going. And what on earth did you need a sleeping bag for? Your message was so cryptic." But T.C. did not reply. He retreated back into the room and Tessa saw him opening the top drawer of her bureau. "Hey, what are you doing?" She ran in after him.

"Packing. Didn't I tell you I'd take you camping on the ridge?" He continued to rummage through her drawer, pulling out a T-shirt, a pair of jeans, and two pairs of silky underwear.

Tessa grabbed them from his hands. "You did mention it, but you didn't say it would be tonight. I mean...don't you have to plan for these things? Have you got a tent? What about food? And...." She turned around and looked out at the twilight. "It'll be dark before we get anywhere!" she wailed.

T.C. smiled. "Listen to you. Since when does an overnight in the woods have to be planned like a military expedition. You bring a sleeping bag, a change of clothes, and you go!" He reached out and took the underwear back. "And so what if it's dark?"

"Well, how do you know there won't be bears?"

She looked so forlorn that he threw back his head and laughed. "Bears? You really *are* scared! Tessa, the Gemini Lakes may be many things, a wildlife sanctuary among them, but any bears that were in the region hightailed it out of here fifty years ago when the valley was first flooded. The only wildlife around here is the kind that can fly or climb very high trees."

"Bears can climb trees," she retorted somewhat defiantly, for she did not like being thought a chicken. But T.C., still chuckling, went back to his task. "And anyway, what about dinner?" she inquired. "I'm starved."

He looked at her obliquely from under his thick

lashes. "I brought along a can of beans," he said. "Now let's find a bag for your stuff and hit the road, okay?"

It wasn't the kind of romantic evening Tessa had envisioned, but then she realized it would be hard to fulfill that vision out here in Choate, where there wasn't even a diner open after 8:00 P.M., much less a romantic restaurant with a fireplace and strolling violinists.

Still, she couldn't pass up the opportunity to drive T.C.'s little Fiat, which she did with a panache he seemed to enjoy. He didn't even flinch when she took some narrow turns at a speed distinctly above the legal limit.

"Okay, Mario Andretti," he said at last, "the turn-off is here. Watch it—it's a dirt access road, and it comes up fast."

He was right. Suddenly there was a gap in the hedges, filled only with black night. Tessa began to turn, quailed at the darkness, and the Fiat stalled.

His eyes glowed with humor in the dim interior light of the car. "Want me to take over?"

Tessa narrowed her eyes and tried to peer past the halogen headlights into the wall of black brush in front of the car. "We're going in there?"

"Tessa. Have you ever camped out before?"

"Sure." She would not meet his eyes. "In summer camp. Once. When I was thirteen."

T.C. snorted good-naturedly and got out. He walked around to her side as Tessa, unwilling to leave the cozy comfort of the car, maneuvered herself over the stick shift and into the passenger seat. T.C.

started the car and began to plow slowly through the night.

"This is an access road to one of the old dams," he said. "It'll take us up to the north end of the ridge, about three miles away from the construction." He smiled. "You'll like it up there." He took his hand off the stick shift and covered Tessa's. "No bears."

"No bears." Tessa grinned at him, and turned to look out the window. She felt idiotic for having seemed frightened. Now the night seemed full of velvet welcome, and she watched with interest as the bush on either side of the road gave way to stands of oak and maple. She could smell the sharp scent of pine on the air and, beneath it, the clear tang of fresh water. She was glad to be there with T.C.

The road rose and bent, and suddenly they were in a tiny clearing. T.C. turned off the ignition but left the headlights on so Tessa could see. There was a small patch of ground that sloped gently down from the spot where they had parked. Off to one side was a tiny brick building, looking like a dollhouse with a gabled roof and dark-green trim. The doors and windows were boarded up with weathered wood.

Beyond the house, slightly to the right, the ground sloped off more steeply, and in the moonlight that was just appearing in the east above the trees Tessa could see silver slashes of water among the branches.

T.C. reached into the compartment behind his seat and pulled out a large flashlight. Then he switched off the headlights, and for a moment they were surrounded by darkness. But it was a benign darkness, and when T.C. switched on the light he saw that

Tessa was smiling. "Ready to set up camp, pardner?" he asked.

"Ready," she replied. He leaned forward and placed a single gentle kiss on her mouth.

"Great. You gather the firewood. I'll unroll the sleeping bags. That sound fair to you?"

Of course she would not let him get away with that, and in the end they did all the work together, laughing and joking as they worked. It took about half an hour to get the fire going and the supplies unpacked. Tessa was delighted to see that T.C. had gone considerably beyond the tin of beans he had led her to expect, although by that point the beans would have been fine. From a nylon duffel bag he brought out a loaf of thick country bread, a slab of flaky cheddar cheese, and, to Tessa's amazement, a breast of smoked turkey. Then he unpacked two plates, real silverware and a bottle of good red wine. There were even two wineglasses, which he had delicately wrapped in two face towels.

"This is what's known as improving on nature," he informed her solemnly as their glasses clinked together. They were both reclining against a large piece of deadwood T.C. had dragged into the clearing, using the sleeping bags as cushions. Tessa felt as if she were dwelling in the lap of luxury rather than roughing it in the great outdoors. The June air was silky and fragrant, and the silence, except for the crackle of the fire, was like liquid. The water was a gentle presence in her mind, so still and pure and patient.

"How much water is there in Choate I?" she asked.

"Well, the reservoir pumps 300 million gallons a day into the MWC pipes without lowering the water level. That's enough to flood the city of Boston under three feet of water. The entire reservoir contains about 412 billion gallons of water—the largest untreated body of drinking water in the country."

Tessa whistled softly between her teeth. "That's a lot of H_2O. Do we need it all?"

"That and more. That's why we're creating the Gemini Lakes. When we open up the aqueduct along the south ridge, we'll be creating a basin for an additional 300 billion gallons. That's more than enough to meet the increased demands for the next two hundred years."

"But where will all that water come from?"

"Same place it comes from now. The rain, the rivers, the mountain streams in the Berkshires. It'll just have more space to fill up."

"But what if there isn't enough water to fill two reservoirs? You said yourself a dry season could be devastating."

T.C. thought for a moment before answering her question. "It'll take years," he said, "but the Gemini Lakes will fill."

"How do you *know* that?" Tessa could not help her persistence. It was important to her that T.C. explain the source of his confidence, the source of his commitment to this project. Her curiosity from a professional standpoint as a reporter was intensified by her urgent desire to get to the bottom of Thomas Chimatsu.

"I know," he said patiently, "because it's my job to

know." Then, as if aware that his answer did not begin to satisfy her needs, he reached into his nylon knapsack and pulled out a book. "Have you seen this yet?" he asked.

Shaking her head, she reached out and took it from him. It was a small hardcover, very old, and the binding had faded into illegibility. But opening the flyleaf, Tessa read, "*Choate Hollow. The Town that Time Forgot.*" She looked up at T.C.

"I know," he said ruefully. "Corny title. Read on."

Tessa leafed slowly through the book, pausing to stare at the sepia photographs of the small country town. The houses were clustered in a bowl of land that gently sloped up to the surrounding mountains. A white, steepled church and rambling wooden mill rose from the center of the bowl, and the entire scene looked as still and poised as the waters she felt behind her on the ridge.

"But what about the people?" she mused aloud.

"Yes, what about the people? They mostly went to other towns, big cities.... Some of them even worked on the project for the water commission. It was the Depression, you know."

But Tessa was not listening. She was reading a passage from the back of the book, and now she reread it aloud. It was a quote from a local newspaper dated in June of 1938. "'A hush fell over the town hall tonight as the first note of the clock sounded midnight. The town was officially dissolved as of that moment. The orchestra faintly sounded the strains of "Auld Lang Syne." Muffled sounds of sobbing were heard, and hardened men were not ashamed to take out their handkerchiefs.'"

She looked up to find T.C. watching her closely. His expression was at once ardent and sad, and she felt that she had just shared a very intimate moment with him. But she could not fathom his point of view. How could a man like T.C., who obviously cared so much, continue to work on a project where people were getting displaced, just as they had in the old Choate Hollow? Or was it that he didn't really care about the people? That was a possibility that Tessa did not care to entertain. The repercussions as far as her own as yet unnamed feelings for T.C. were too great.

So to cover her confusion she turned idly back to the flyleaf of the book. There, for the first time, she saw the name inscribed in it. "'Beryl McGregor,'" she read. "'June, 1942.'" She looked up, shocked. "This is Beryl's book! How did you get Beryl's book?"

"She gave it to me." T.C. leaned forward and stirred the logs into a more comfortable blaze.

"She gave it to you? You know Beryl McGregor?"

"Is that so surprising? It is a small town, and I've been working out here for months, you know."

His blandness unnerved her. "But when? I mean, how could you...I would think," she concluded lamely, "that you two people would be the last two to meet, let alone exchange books. I would think you'd be on opposite sides of the fence."

T.C. did not blink as he gazed at her. "There are no fences, Tessa. There's only the truth. The truth, in this case, is that the Gemini Lakes will exist, just like Choate Hollow once existed. Beryl knows the truth as well as I do." T.C. turned to look out at the water through the trees.

"How do you know Beryl feels that way?" Tessa demanded. "Did she tell you how she feels about losing her home?"

"Did she tell you?" The reply was a challenge, offered so immediately that Tessa was sure T.C. knew her interview with Beryl had been unproductive. She wished he weren't so intuitive. But deep down she felt that Beryl did not want to lose the house, and that she would be willing to fight for it if the opportunity presented itself. She looked up at T.C. and met the challenge with her own level gaze. "No, she didn't tell me anything," she said. "But I think she'll fight for that house."

"And do you think she's right to?"

This question took Tessa by surprise. "Right? Well, I guess I've never really thought about it that way. It doesn't matter what I think, anyway. I'm just here to cover the story. There is no right or wrong as far as I'm concerned."

"Exactly my point." This seemed to be what T.C. wanted to hear, for he now leaned back against the sleeping bag with a satisfied smile on his lips.

"But you're in a different position," Tessa said. Somehow she wanted to press him on this point, to test his commitment and see how deep it went. Because if he was committed to his ideas then it stood to reason that he could be committed to people as well. "For someone in your position, I would think there are very clear lines of right or wrong. You care about what happens to the environment, you care about preserving natural beauties. I would think you—"

"You would think I what?"

Tessa shook her head. There was something dangerous in the way he tossed out the question. "I don't know. I guess I would expect you to—just care one way or the other."

T.C.'s hand reached out and tipped her chin up so that she had to meet his eyes. "But I do care one way or the other, Tessa," he said softly. "That's just the point. I care very much what happens."

To what, she wanted to ask. To Beryl McGregor, or the Gemini Lakes project . . . or to us? But his face was too close to hers to permit speech, and his expression too compelling. She felt herself falling into the deep pools of his gaze just as she had imagined being enveloped by the deep pools of the water beyond the trees. Her body leaned forward toward his as if it knew what was important, even if her mind did not. The issue of the Gemini Lakes and Beryl McGregor seemed the least important thing in the world.

"Come lie with me," T.C. murmured, and held out his arms.

With a sigh of relief, she slipped into his embrace. Their mouths, coming together in passion, canceled out all the questions that lay unanswered between them. This was the simple truth, thought Tessa, who was feeling the anxiety slip away from her in a rush of exhaled breath: that the power of their attraction should wipe out all the confusing details of their lives, reducing their connection to one tenuous but indestructible thread. This was all that mattered now.

T.C.'s lips on hers were hungry and urgent, and Tessa felt her body melt against his with a rush of heat, as if her limbs had become molded plastic. Their tongues sought each other urgently and soon became locked in a network of increasing depth and complexity. Tessa felt the hard pearls of his teeth raking at her lower lip, and she stretched her chin upward so that the combined pressures of hot tongue and hard teeth could travel down the slope of her neck to the base of her throat. With consummate skill, T.C. was playing her body like a violin, tuning each string of her being with deliberation, so that, as he moved along the planes of her collarbone and into the declivity between her breasts, she felt herself growing tauter and sharper with desire.

Now their clothing had become a hindrance, and they removed it quickly, tossing it just outside the circle of light and moving closer to the warmth of the fire. They knelt facing each other, breathing deeply of the mixed scent of burning wood and acrid pine needles. The night air was cool, but not uncomfortable. She delighted in the way her nipples slowly hardened and rose in the exposed air, and she could feel her belly shifting with desire.

T.C.'s body was responding to his own growing passion. Slowly, making certain that every movement was exactly right for both of them, Tessa reached out for him. He was hard and warm and as he bent his head to her breasts she could feel a shudder of containment pass through him. His mouth teased the tip of one breast and then closed around it, and he raised one hand so that it covered the entire surface of the other. His free hand reached around and caressed the curve of her buttocks, fingers drumming gently against the small of her back. Tessa felt liquid fire moving up her spine, branching off until her entire body was warm and loose.

His mouth moved away from her breast then and began a deliberate descent down the course of her ribs and belly. Tessa arched forward, only vaguely aware that she was completely exposed to the night and any creature—human or otherwise—that might venture to their little clearing. But Tessa felt herself completely opened up to the elements. She was at one with the world, and all the world was T.C.

Again and again T.C. led her gently back from the brink, each time coming closer to the edge, then moving back with consummate control. Tessa felt the tension threaten to explode within her at the flooding ebb and flow of desire, and she writhed beneath T.C.'s golden body. At one point, he lifted his head from her belly and whispered, "Relax. We have all night. We have the world."

Tessa shuddered and laughed shakily. Conversation did not come easily to her during lovemaking, and certainly not when she was so close to the edge. "But I want to...I want to be together now—completely."

T.C. smiled and shifted his position. "Tessa." His eyes were large with passion and an amused wonder. "You want to know everything, to understand everything. You are insatiable." He laughed crookedly and raised his body above hers, pausing just at the point of entry. "You are a mirror into my soul," he added, and his voice sounded fierce.

She looked up at him, momentarily diverted by his strange choice of words. Searching his face, she found a trace of something besides desire on his features. Was it sorrow? Pain? Her thoughts dissolved at once as, with a deep moan, T.C. pressed his lips against hers and entered her at the same time.

Each time it had been unique. Tessa knew that. And yet, this time as they rocked together toward fulfillment, she was aware of a special sensation. T.C.'s body was pressed tightly against hers, and the fusion of flesh and limb was almost complete. But just at that blinding moment when the bottom dropped out from under her, she felt that he was not only caressing her—he was clinging to her as well. And she was clinging to him, too—as if her life depended on it, and it surely did, because he took her to such heights that she cried out in fear and joy.

Afterward, as they lay against the mat of pine and moss that had been their bed, she could not be sure who had cried out. The climax had come in shuddering waves of sensation and had kept on coming, as if the tides T.C. had stemmed for so long had gathered into a furious series of waves, each one more stunning than the next. And it took a long time to recover, so that by the time the sky righted itself above them and the earth below she had almost convinced herself that she had imagined the outcry.

Still, he seemed different to her now. She glanced

over to where he lay, his profile etched against the now-dim glow of the flames. She felt she had glimpsed an inner Thomas Chimatsu, a part very deep beneath the self-possessed exterior.

When he turned to her, however, his smile was complete and without any shadow of turmoil. "Do you know," he said, reaching out one hand to trace a lazy pattern against her cheek, "I've never made love outdoors before."

"Ho! And you had the nerve to tease me for my lack of experience. I thought you did it all the time."

He chucked her lightly under the chin. "You know I don't. And I don't camp out all the time, either. I like my creature comforts." He leaned back and stretched like a cat. "But that. . . . Now that was a creature comfort." He chuckled. "No, that was more. That was very, very special."

Tessa smiled. "Very, very," she murmured, fitting herself once more into the crook of his upraised arm. She felt exquisitely satisfied—so much so that she didn't want to think about the niggling point that he had not said *she* was special. Part of her appreciated T.C.'s attitude—surely it was what she herself wanted from this relationship right now. But part of her longed for terms of endearment, for words of commitment. She could not bring herself to say the words herself, so she knew she would have to be content with repeating his phrase. "Very, very special."

T.C. cocked his head to look down at her. "I bet those bears were pretty impressed," he told her. In spite of herself, Tessa squealed and cuddled closer to him.

"You rat! Now I'm shivering." She looked around the circle of darkness that enveloped them. "You don't think anyone—or anything—is out there, do you?"

He laughed. "No, you goose, of course not. The only things out there are things that are more scared of you than you are of them."

"Wanna bet?"

He sat up. "Come on. Get into this sleeping bag and I'll stoke the fire. A good blaze will do wonders for your courage—and those goose bumps."

She pulled the sleeping bag around her and sat with her knees drawn up against her chest, watching as he added logs and fanned the blaze to life. Again she was struck by the grace of his gestures, and by the unselfconscious way he moved, even without clothing. He was very sure about everything he did.

"T.C.," she asked, "what did you and Beryl McGregor have to say to each other?"

He turned around and smiled. "I went there to try and talk her out of refusing to leave," he said simply.

Tessa's eyes widened. "You did?"

"Well, I tried. She was very polite, but she made it quite clear that it was not a subject that was up for discussion." He shrugged and went back to his task. "So we talked about other things. I liked her a lot." He paused for a moment. "We liked each other."

Tessa felt a stab of envy. She could imagine the two of them talking and liking each other a lot. They both had the same obliqueness—the same self-confident gestures, the same air of containment without hostility. "Wasn't it kind of awkward, your being

somewhat responsible for her predicament?" She
could not keep the edge of irritation out of her voice,
even though she was ashamed of it.

He turned to face her with that patient half smile.
"It wasn't a problem at all," he said. "I knew she was
committed to her point of view, and it had nothing to
do with me or what I do."

"But don't you feel bad about taking her home
from her?" It was a question asked in exasperation,
and Tessa regretted it. Earlier she had told him that it
didn't matter to her, but she had been wrong. It did
matter—more than she cared to admit. Her anxiety
over T.C.'s apparent lack of regard for Beryl's plight
stemmed from her fears that he might someday dis-
play the same lack of regard for her. She both envied
him his cool composure and hated it. She could also
identify herself with it. Hadn't she been just as
detached about Douglas?

T.C. watched her face, wondering how he could
set this woman's mind at rest without saying more
than he felt prepared to say. "I'll tell you what," he
said suddenly. "Let's go see Beryl together. It might
answer your question—seeing the two of us together
with no hostility between us."

For a moment Tessa thought of protesting that he
didn't have to go to that length to prove his integrity.
But she was enough of a journalist to know a great
story when it stared her in the face. To have the chief
engineer and the lone holdout together in the same
room was too good an opportunity to refuse. "Sounds
great to me," she said, careful to keep her enthusiasm
under guard. "But do you think she'll really talk with

me there? She seemed kind of closemouthed the other day."

"I think she'll be glad to see us there together. And I think she needs to talk now. She's trying to get a court-ordered delay, and she must realize she could use the publicity at this point."

"When are they scheduled to start demolition if she doesn't get the delay?" Tessa asked.

"Tuesday, June 17," T.C. told her.

Tessa gasped. "The seventeenth? But that's the same day the original Choate Hollow was evacuated!"

T.C. smiled ruefully. "I know. The irony is too heavy to believe, isn't it?"

Tessa was shaking her head. "It's also," she said, "my birthday."

9

TESSA OPENED HER EYES. A faint crackling sound had awakened her, but she couldn't see where it had come from. Everything was gray. She blinked, trying to recall where she was. Then she remembered, and the fact that everything was gray hit home with a shock. She was out in the woods. In the fog. And there was no one in the sleeping bag with her.

Making an effort to control the panic that stiffened her limbs, she sat up. "T.C.?" Her voice quavered. "Hey, T.C., where are you?"

Instead of a reply, a disembodied arm appeared out of the smoke-colored wall before her eyes. At the end of the arm was a cup of something steaming and hot. Tessa took it gratefully and sipped, trying to pierce through the fog to find the rest of T.C.'s body. "What is going on?" she croaked. "What happened to the great outdoors?"

She heard a rustle, and then his face appeared before her as if swimming in mist. "Just morning fog," he said, kissing her forehead above the steaming coffee mug. "It'll burn off in a few minutes, you'll see."

"I *hope* I'll see. It looks to me as if I'll never see again." She shook her head and tried to refocus. T.C.

was right. The circle of trees around the little clearing was becoming faintly visible, and the gray was getting a shade lighter.

"I thought camping was supposed to be fun," she groaned. "How can you see the great outdoors if you're blinded by fog?"

"Come on, quit complaining. I didn't notice you crawling around in the predawn gloom to gather logs for a morning fire. Where do you think that hot coffee came from—Mr. Coffee?"

Tessa snuggled back into the warmth of the sleeping bag with a sigh. "I don't care where it came from—it's delicious. And thank you for getting up, although I must admit I was disappointed to wake up without you beside me." She reached out for his hand. "I was sort of looking forward to it."

T.C. took the coffee mug out of her hand and stretched out on top of her, outside of the sleeping bag. "So was I," he murmured against her hair. "But you were hogging the bag so badly I had to get out." He stabbed her with a finger between the ribs and she doubled up with laughter.

"I did not! Ouch! Hey, quit it, I'm . . . not . . . ticklish!"

"Then stop giggling!" They tussled good-naturedly for a while and Tessa would have liked it to develop into something more amorous, but T.C. refused.

"Not that I wouldn't love to crawl back in there with you, but we have work to do."

"Work to do? But it's Saturday!"

T.C. made a face. "I thought you reporters were so dedicated you always worked on Saturdays."

"Humph." Tessa pretended annoyance, but she remembered a time when she had insisted exactly that to T.C. She knew he remembered too. "Who do you expect me to interview out here in the middle of the wilderness—the squirrels?" She saw him grin and grinned back. "And no spooky comments about the bears, either—you can't scare me in the light of day. Such as it is." The fog was lifting further, and Tessa could see the old mill house hovering in the morning mist to her left. More light was visible through the trees.

"We're not going to interview a bear," T.C. said. "Although I expect Beryl McGregor has been called worse things in her seventy-two years."

"Beryl! I forgot!" Tessa sat up so fast that she nearly knocked T.C. backward. "That's right, we're going to see her today. Oh, Lord, I've got to get myself together. I can't botch this interview like I did yesterday—I know she won't give me a third chance. Do you really think she'll talk to us? Together? Is she really seventy-two? She doesn't look it, that's for sure. . . . I've got to get back to the motel and clean up—I can't go in there looking like this—and I need my tape recorder."

This remarkable speech was delivered while Tessa, in a flurry of activity, yanked herself out of the sleeping bag and into her clothes. Now she paused and looked down at T.C., who was watching her with amusement. "Come on, I thought you said we had work to do. Let's go."

He smiled. "I doubt if even Beryl McGregor is ready to receive visitors at this hour," he told her.

"Why? What time is it?" Tessa looked around as if she would be able to calculate the hour by the position of the not-yet-visible sun.

"It's five forty-five," T.C. informed her.

"Five forty—are you kidding? You got me up at five forty-five?" She sank slowly to the ground, exhausted by the mere thought of it.

But T.C. stood up and pulled her after him. "Come on, where's your pioneer spirit? We've got lots to do before we leave here. We've got to break camp, and I want to check something down by the old valley dam a mile or so along the ridge. And you're right—even Beryl McGregor will not receive us looking like this, so we'll have to go back to your place and shower and change. Come on, let's get going!"

Tessa sighed elaborately and began to roll up their gear. "Of all the men I could have met," she complained to the lightening sky, "I had to find a wilderness freak who gets up before the birds."

But, once awake, she was as eager to explore as he was, and after dousing the fire carefully and storing their gear in the Fiat they took off on an hour's walk that proved as delightful as it was informative. T.C. was indeed a wilderness "freak," if the term defined a man who was expert in the flora and fauna of the area. He stopped to point out tiny flowers growing amid the piny carpet of the forest floor and led her to the banks of the reservoir to show her where beavers had built an ingenious dam. Once, they saw a flock of Canada geese dawdling along the way back up north, and T.C. spotted one of the bald eagles that had found refuge in the Choate preserve.

"There's been talk of opening up Choate for more recreational activities," he told her as they threaded their way along the ridge, now splashed with sunshine. "But I don't think the environmentalists will let them get away with it." He stooped down to finger a handful of soil and looked up into a tree above them. "See? See that?" He drew Tessa to him and directed her gaze to a branch of the tree. "That's a golden eagle nest up there. See it?"

Tessa could barely see the thatch of twigs that he referred to. "Yes, I see. Why would the environmentalists not want recreational camping out here? What harm could a few skiers and campers do in this huge wilderness?"

T.C. shrugged. "Not much harm if they're regulated carefully. But the bald eagles would never stand for it. They're very private creatures. They'd simply leave, and there's really no place else suitable for them to go. Choate contains the largest population of bald eagles in New England." He took one last look up into the tree before moving on. "It's better to leave it alone."

Tessa looked after him. How strange that he should be saying that—he who was involved in a project that was causing massive upheaval on the south shore of the reservoir. She wondered if he was aware of the contradictions he presented. But now was not the time to bring it up. It was turning out to be a beautiful morning, and T.C. had apparently forgotten what he had said as he stopped to measure the water level by a defunct earthen dam along the ridge.

By the time they got back to the car, the sun was

burning in the eastern sky, and Tessa was ravenously hungry. They stopped at the diner where she had had dinner with Paul on her first night in the Hollow. Although it was only six-thirty in the morning the diner was full of homey bustle, and T.C. and Tessa ate heartily while they talked to one of the waitresses about the reservoir project. Both of them ducked their heads to cover a smile when the waitress referred to the project as "the Gemini Lakes."

After breakfast they went back to Tessa's motel room to shower and change. Instead of showering together, which would surely have led to a delightful, if time-consuming interlude, they took turns in the bathroom while the other stayed in the room making phone calls and organizing the day. At first Tessa was put off by T.C.'s suggestion that she "go ahead and change while I make some business calls," but then she decided she liked the intimacy it implied. That they were lovers was indisputable—that they were also two professionals who could go about their business and avoid obvious distractions was a pleasant surprise. She took a quick shower, humming quietly to herself and pretending that she and T.C. were an old but happily married couple for whom this sort of thing was commonplace. Well, she told herself, there was no harm in a simple daydream, was there?

T.C. had offered to call Beryl and arrange the interview, but Tessa had insisted that it was her responsibility. She was feeling her journalistic courage returning full force, and she didn't want T.C.—or Beryl—to think that she had to rely on someone else to set up a successful interview. For she was determined that this one be successful.

Beryl agreed to see her that morning without hesitation. Nor did she seem surprised when Tessa asked if it was all right for Mr. Chimatsu to come along.

"Of course," Beryl had said. "T.C. is welcome anytime."

"She said you're welcome anytime," she reported to T.C. when he came out of the bathroom. He was fully dressed in a pair of neat dark chinos and a button-down shirt. His hair was slicked softly back across his forehead, and he smelled faintly of pungent after-shave. She resisted the urge to go up and slip her arms around his waist.

"A gracious lady," said T.C. and dropped a kiss on Tessa's damp hair as he bent to peer critically at himself in the mirror over the desk where she sat. "Two gracious ladies. Ready to go? And this time I get to drive."

When they got to Beryl's place they found her working in the small flower garden that ran along the front wall of the house. She stood up to wave to them and then returned to her work. Seeing her again, Tessa wondered what it was that had made it so difficult for her to interview the woman yesterday. She looked so harmless and pleasant, crouched there beside the tulip and hyacinth stalks. This time, Tessa promised herself, she would ask the right questions no matter what.

Beryl led them into the kitchen, where coffee waited. The day was warm and the back door was propped open. The garden was alive with the smells and sounds of early summer.

"Miss McGregor—Beryl," Tessa began after a few minutes of pleasant chatting. "I know we've been talking a lot about what life used to be like around here. But what about right now? What is it like for you now? Are you sorry about having to leave?"

Beryl's eyes met hers with a cool blue gaze. "Of course I'm sorry," she said softly. "This is my home."

"Are you still planning to fight the demolition order?"

Beryl smiled briefly, as if she had been anticipating this question. She rummaged in her pocket and pulled out a piece of paper, which she handed across the kitchen table to Tessa. "I'm still fighting," she said.

"This is a court-ordered delay!" Tessa read it and passed it to T.C. She looked at Beryl with new respect. "You got them to stop the demolition!"

Beryl nodded. "But only for a few days. Only so they can't tear down my house before the superior court judge has made his decision. If he decides against me—again—then it'll happen on Friday." She blinked and Tessa understood the bitterness Beryl was suppressing.

"Beryl, you must know that it won't work. The courts have already decided in favor of the Metropolitan Water Commission once—what makes you think they'll change their decision?" Tessa's voice was as gentle as she could make it.

Beryl shook her head. "What they think—what they decide—has nothing to do with it. I have to do this. I have no choice." Now she turned to T.C. "You understand," she said. "Don't you?"

Tessa watched the two of them. For the first time she was able to see them as adversaries. Neither one of them looked angry, but she could sense the implacable contest of wills battling beneath those two steady gazes. How, she wondered, could two such obvious adversaries think of themselves as friends? What was it that enabled T.C. and Beryl to maintain such a distance between their personal feelings and their deep beliefs? Did it mean that they had some secret power or skill Tessa lacked, even with her supposed detachment from emotional issues? Or were they more easily able to commit themselves to a cause than to a person?

She looked from one to the other. No, she decided, those were not the faces of people who lacked commitment. They were dispassionate when it came to issues such as the one that divided them now—but they were clearly committed. Her gaze rested on T.C. She knew that there was a lot going on beneath that steady gaze of his. Those composed features hid a mind that was working like a computer even if he didn't show it. And they hid a man of deep feelings, too. Just looking at him, she was able to envision the man who had risen above her last night in a transport of erotic fury. Tessa felt her thighs heat beneath her clothing, and she looked away from T.C. with an effort. Beryl, too, seemed still and composed. But Beryl was also hiding a flurry of thoughts and feelings beneath that serene expression. The question was, what were they both withholding? And what did it have to do with her—Tessa Drew? She felt drawn into their struggle and knew she had to commit herself to this story, to hitch her star to one of these two people, so remarkably alike and yet so different from anyone Tessa had ever known. She had to pick a side, even though as a reporter she had never allowed herself to do so before. The question was, on which side of the fence should she sit?

Beryl, who had been watching Tessa observing T.C., chose this moment to speak. "I want you to help me on this," she said calmly. "I intend to fight to save this house. And exposure through your TV station can help, can't it?"

Tessa nodded, not trusting herself to speak. She could almost feel the pull of these two strong-willed people as they fought silently over Tessa's allegiance. Her palms were damp with sweat.

Her first allegiance, she knew, would be to T.C. One did not spend nights of love with a man like that without it counting for something, she thought. But then she remembered the chill that had gone through her when T.C. had told her that, despite his friendship with Beryl, he would do everything in his power to get her to give up the house. That counted for something, too. She had to choose between the commitment of her heart, and the logic of her mind. What, she wondered, would T.C. do in this situation?

It was at that moment that Tessa realized she was going to align herself on Beryl's side of the struggle. Not only because she embraced Beryl's point of view more fully than she did T.C.'s, but because she wanted to prove something to T.C. and to herself. She had to prove to him that she, too, could be totally professional, despite their relationship. And the longer Beryl held out, the better the story Tessa had.

There was another reason behind her decision. Tessa also had to prove to herself that she didn't care as much about T.C. as she suspected. She was so tempted to lose herself in his strength, in his power over her. T.C.'s lack of emotion about Beryl frightened her. If he could be this detached about Beryl, mightn't he also lack emotion where Tessa was concerned?

As she was thinking this she turned and found that T.C.'s eyes were trained on her face. It seemed to Tessa, in that pregnant moment of silence, that he must have known what she was thinking—known of her sudden resolve to help Beryl and, even worse, why. For a moment they stared at each other—strangers, yet acutely aware of what the other was thinking. *He knows what I'm going to do,* she thought, amazed at her own certainty. *And he isn't going to try and stop me.* She looked at him. *I might know how he feels about the Gemini Lakes, but I don't know how he feels about me. But we're obviously on opposite sides of the battle now, from this moment on.*

The silence in the kitchen grew. Tessa looked back at Beryl, who was watching her patiently, waiting for her decision. She nodded, and Beryl nodded back, as if she understood what had brought Tessa to her resolution. Tessa dared not look at T.C. as she spoke. He, too, would know why she answered as she did. "I'll help you, Beryl," she said, and her voice seemed to echo on the still summer air.

T.C. stirred for the first time in his chair. "I hope you know what you're doing, Beryl," he said. Although Tessa was aware of the genuine concern in his voice, she was annoyed at him for directing his statement at Beryl and not at her. Didn't she count for something in this discussion? But she was enough of a professional to automatically adjust her tape recorder so that she could catch the words of her two antagonists.

"I think I know what I'm doing," Beryl said with a little smile. "But thanks for your concern, T.C."

T.C. returned the smile with a small nod. "I *am* concerned for you—you know that. But I want you to know that the court delay—and Tessa's intervention—is not going to help." He nodded in Tessa's direction without looking at her.

"You can't be sure of that," Beryl said. "Why, for all you know, your Gemini Lakes might be in for a five-year dry spell."

For the first time, Tessa heard the tension in T.C.'s voice. "They're not *my* Gemini Lakes. And we're not in for a dry spell. Your own almanac says it's going to be the wettest year in a century."

"They may not be your Gemini Lakes," Beryl replied. "But it *is* my house. You understand, T.C."

T.C. nodded and stood up. "Yes," he said, "I do." He looked directly at Tessa for the first time, and she thought she saw a plea in his eyes. He even made a move toward her as if to take her hand in his. His eyes caressed her face, and he wore that half smile she found so irresistible. Of course he cared about

Beryl McGregor, she suddenly knew. And of course he cared—even more—about her!

But she realized that T.C. would not consider taking her hand in his or displaying any sign of their personal relationship while in a professional situation.

"Are you coming?" he asked her.

"No," she replied, her heart aching to say otherwise. "I'm not."

T.C. nodded. "Well, I suppose you two have work to do. And I've got to get back up to the site. I'm sure Commissioner Conklin will be waiting for me if he's heard about this little delay." He took a few steps out of the room and turned. "Oh, Tessa, this will leave you without a way back into town. Can you manage, or shall I send someone to pick you up?"

Tessa felt like shouting, "Send someone? What about you? What about us?" But she controlled the impulse. "It's all right," she said evenly. "I'm probably going to be busy until late this evening. And I'll be getting a camera crew out here, too. I'll manage. Don't worry about me."

T.C.'s jaw tightened, but his voice was calm. "I won't worry," he said, and then he walked out the door.

Tessa was grateful that Beryl did not remark on T.C. in any way after he left. She did not know how she would have responded if she had. But before long they were deeply involved in plans and discussions taking all of Tessa's attention.

Apparently word of Beryl's court-ordered delay had gotten around, and with it the expectation that fireworks would surely follow. In the next few hours

the phone began to ring madly. Reporters all the way
from Boston were calling to see if they could come
out and talk to the little old lady who was trying to
stop the Gemini Lakes project.

Beryl was very polite on the phone, telling them all
that she was only talking to one reporter and they
would have to learn the latest developments on the
Channel 8 news. Tessa couldn't help feeling a shiver
of smug delight at the thought of scooping her colleagues, and she knew that Tim McNulty and the
executives at the station were smacking their lips in
anticipation of high viewer shares and revenues.

Tessa had called the station and explained what
had happened, and they had fallen all over themselves to help her in any way possible. Tim even
called her back from his home, and she knew *he*
never worked on weekends if he could help it.

"What do you need?" he had asked. "A camera
crew? You want remote equipment? I can send out a
producer to help you organize the report if you like."

"No, no," Tessa said, "that won't be necessary.
Just Paul, and the remote technician—and more tape
cassettes, please."

"Right, right, of course." There was a pause on the
line. "Tessa," Tim began hesitantly. "You know this
could be a terrific story—a great story, an award
winner. You know that, don't you?"

Tessa grinned. She was enjoying this. "Yes, Tim,
I'm aware of that. Look, Beryl's waiting, so I've got
to go. You stick by that phone today in case I need
you, you hear?"

"Sure thing. Good luck, Tessa."

She hung up and rolled her eyes at Beryl. "You're a star already, Beryl," she said softly. "There's no publicity like refusing publicity."

"You're a star too, Tessa," replied Beryl, and Tessa knew there was something of a challenge in that statement.

"Well, let's get started," Tessa suggested. "My photographer won't be here until this afternoon. I want to spend the morning getting everything on audiotape—the history of the house, your history and, most important, a blow-by-blow account of the MWC's move to take the land." She pulled another blank cassette from her bag. "Where do you want to begin?"

"At the beginning," replied Beryl, and she did. She talked about growing up in the Smith River Valley, as the area that had been covered by Choate I had been called. She recollected that as a very young child she had heard grown-ups talking about the state breathing down their necks for their land.

"Since the turn of the century, people were talking about the Smith River Valley as a doomed place," she said. "It had never really gotten off the ground as a manufacturing area, and there wasn't anything major to keep people here. The population began to thin out during the First World War and it never really built back up again." Beryl paused, her eyes focused on some remote spot in her own history. "I remember coming back here in '38," she said in a soft voice. "It was so strange, standing in the middle of the town where I had known so many people and having no point of reference." She shook her head slightly. "Actually, there was one building left standing. The town hall, a big brick building, was standing there in the middle of this vast tract of land, bare and empty as a desert except for the water and mud. A town hall, standing there without any town at all."

By late afternoon, Paul Manning had arrived, and while Paul followed Beryl around, Tessa sat at the huge kitchen table and edited her notes. She had been allotted three minutes of live air time for the Saturday evening news—an unheard-of amount on such short notice, and especially on a weekend news program where the cost of field reporting was usually cut down because of the smaller audience.

At five-thirty the technician arrived from the station to hook the remote equipment up for the broadcast. He was over an hour late, and the next forty-five minutes were spent in a frenzy of activity arranging cables, checking for sound and light and checking the cues for the switches from live to taped material. Tessa, who was used to the chaotic deluge of last-minute details, hurried around in a state of controlled hysteria, but she was very much aware of Beryl, who sat primly in her armchair in the living room, watching every move she made with guarded concentration.

At six twenty-five, the red light beamed over Paul's camera, and Tessa was on the air.

"Good evening. This is Tessa Drew for the WBOS Focus Team, reporting to you from Choate Hollow. I am sitting in the home of Miss Beryl McGregor—a lovely and gracious home belonging to a lovely and gracious woman. But this home, which has been in this wooded hollow since Miss McGregor's grandfather built it a hundred years ago, will not be standing much longer. If the MWC has its way—and there is every indication that the district judge will rule in its favor—this home will go under the bulldozer's blade in less than a week's time. This woman will lose her home so that you can have a bit more water for your nightly bath."

Tessa was well aware that she was playing flagrantly on her viewers' emotions, and particularly on their sense of guilt. But she was relying on Beryl herself to balance this image of the helpless little old lady being dispossessed. She was counting on whetting the viewers' interest even further by exploiting Beryl's strong determination in the face of the inevitable. And Beryl handled herself beautifully. She was neither piteous nor crotchety, and Tessa knew her intriguing personality would be an important part of the effectiveness of the story.

She had never allowed herself to get so carried away by a story before—not even in the story of the teenage runaways, when she had been well aware of playing on the sympathy of the audience. She knew she would later have to listen to Tim's chortles of delight at her powerful pitch, and to the gentle teasing from her colleagues about going for another Boston Best award.

But she didn't care. Tessa was determined to do this right. She had something to prove. If Thomas Chimatsu wanted to separate life from work, then Tessa Drew would show him how it was done!

It was after eight by the time she finally got ready to leave Beryl's. She arranged to come out again the following day, and then the next, both to get more information for her story and to be there when any new developments cropped up, as they surely would. Already Tim had phoned to say the station had gotten fifteen calls on the Beryl McGregor story—an unprecedented number for a Saturday night in June. Tessa knew she had done a good day's work and prepared to get into Paul's car with a feeling of satisfied exhaustion. But just as she was about to open the car door, she heard a voice calling to her from the darkness.

"Can I give you a lift?" T.C. asked. He was leaning out of the window of his Fiat, which was parked off to the side of the dirt driveway.

Her first thought was to wonder how long he had been there. Her second thought was whether or not he had seen the news.

She leaned into the car. "Listen, Paul," she began, but Paul cut her off with a curt nod.

"Don't bother to explain," he said. "Just make sure you show up for work tomorrow morning." And before she could protest that it wasn't what he thought at all, he grinned wickedly and gunned the engine, leaving her standing there in the dusty drive.

Tessa approached T.C.'s car with mixed emotions. On the one hand, she felt pure delight at the sight of him and at the fact that, despite their cool parting earlier in the day, he had come to pick her up. On the other hand, she was very much aware that the reason for their cool parting still existed. They clearly occupied opposing camps on the issue of Beryl McGregor and the Gemini Lakes, and she wasn't sure how that would affect their time together. Tessa was

learning that separating work from her personal life
was not her strong suit after all.

But T.C. greeted her cheerfully, as if nothing out
of the ordinary had occurred since that morning
when they slept together in the sleeping bag. He
leaned across the seat and kissed her. "I finished early," he said, pulling the car out onto the road. "I
thought I'd take my chances at catching you on the
way out. How'd your day go?"

"Fine, I guess." Tessa had no idea how to respond
to this sudden switch. Was T.C. serious? Did he really expect that, having aligned himself on the opposite
side of a volatile issue, he could simply pick her up,
peck her cheek and ask how the day had gone? Perhaps he really *did* have the ability to separate work
and emotion. Wouldn't it be ironic if, after years of
thinking that *she* was the cool, objective type, it was
now she who cared too much?

She tried to make her voice light. "Did you catch
the six o'clock news?" she asked.

"No, I was still with Commissioner Conklin and
his boys." He reached over and patted her knee. "But
I'm sure you put together a great piece. You and
Beryl together can't go wrong."

She swiveled around in her seat to face him. "How
can you say that?" she asked, surprised at the
vehemence in her own voice. "How can you act so
cavalierly about what is so important to Beryl
McGregor? And how can you act so cavalierly about
the Gemini Lakes? I saw you out there in the woods
this morning—you love this area! How can you be a
part of its destruction?"

T.C. did not answer this flurry of accusations right away. Instead, he slowed the car and finally pulled it off to the side of the road. He let the engine idle for a moment, then turned it off. Slowly, the sounds of the June night came filtering through the open windows, and the hypnotic rhythm of cricket and owl soothed Tessa's rapid heartbeat.

"Tessa. You must understand me. I am not part of its destruction. I am part of its growth—its future. This area is doomed if we don't change it. Ecologically and sociologically it is eroding, just like the Elliott estate land was eroding before we built the sanctuary there."

"Beryl McGregor is not eroding!" Tessa said hotly. "How can you reconcile that with your views on the sanctity of progress over the natural environment?"

He smiled slightly in the half darkness. "My views on Beryl McGregor's future are not what you might think they are. Things are not that simple in this world, natural or otherwise. And in any case, whatever my personal feelings are—on that or any other subject—they have no bearing on the Gemini Lakes. No bearing at all, do you hear?"

"I don't understand what you mean," she said, and she could hear her voice quavering through the night, sounding small and plaintive in the silence.

He leaned a bit closer to her, so that for a moment Tessa thought—hoped—he was going to kiss her. But instead he had moved so that he could watch her face more clearly. "Ah, Tessa," he whispered, his eyes raking across her face as if searching for something special. "I think you know exactly what I mean.

What else do we have to go on right now but our convictions? What else matters but that we have our jobs to do and we must do them right. Personal issues must not interfere."

"Beryl McGregor is about to lose her house. That seems like a fairly personal issue to me!" Tessa spoke angrily, and she knew it was because of what T.C. had said—or, rather, because of what he had not said. If he was referring to their relationship, and she was sure he was, then why didn't he just come right out and say so?

At the same time, she was angry with herself for expecting something of T.C. she was not prepared to do herself. She was the one who had asked for time to think—to work out her past involvements and concentrate on her career. What gave her the right to expect him to commit himself to her? Why had they reached this impasse, with neither of them able to confront the real issue of their own relationship— their reluctance to admit their growing involvement with each other? Instead, they insisted on talking in riddles about other subjects.

She could tell by looking at T.C. that he was angry, too. "Beryl McGregor is just one person, Tessa," he said tightly. "The important thing is the Gemini Lakes project. It must go through. Millions of people depend on it. That's all that should concern us here."

Tessa felt her heart drop. He was not going to go any further, and neither was she. They had to con-fine themselves to a senseless argument about the merits of the Gemini Lakes. "If you feel nothing for

Beryl's predicament," she said sadly, "at least you might think about the land we're sitting on right now. I saw how you love this place, T.C. Doesn't it matter to you that it's going to be destroyed?"

T.C. stared straight out the window of the car. His fingers grasped the steering wheel so hard that even in the darkness she could see his knuckles shine. "I love this place," he said in a tight whisper. "And I love Beryl McGregor. But it has got to be done, and that's all there is to it."

Tessa began to cry. He sounded so hopeless, and there was nothing she could do to unlock that grim fatality in his voice. She could not cry out to him that she was afraid—that if Thomas Chimatsu was able to speak so coldly about Beryl McGregor and the Gemini Lakes—things that he admittedly loved— what would prevent him from being just as cold someday toward Tessa, whom he had not even admitted he cared about? What could she hope for in their relationship if he could never commit himself to caring beyond a certain point. If he could love this place and destroy it, might he not do the same to her?

"Oh, God, Tessa, please...don't cry. There's no reason to cry." T.C., looking as miserable as Tessa felt, tried to put his arm around her shoulder and draw her against him, but Tessa, caught up in her private despair, pulled away.

"Why not? Why shouldn't I cry?" They both knew she wasn't crying about the Gemini Lakes, she thought bitterly. Why couldn't she talk about what was *really* bothering her? Why *couldn't* she?

"Crying won't help," T.C. said softly. "Nothing

will change the way things are. Only the future will
change—and us."

"What's that supposed to mean?" She glared at him
through her tears. "And don't tell me what to do. I'll
cry if I damn well please, and there's nothing you can
say about it."

The petulance of this statement was so apparent
that it required no answer. But she could feel T.C.
stiffen beside her, and she knew that his patience
with the hopeless tangle they had made of themselves
was wearing thin. She stared at him, trying to conjure up the image of the man she knew. Gone was
their beautiful ease and familiarity together, the
smoldering intimacy that knew no boundaries, that
openness that she had never before experienced. The
man beside her seemed a stranger, trapped across the
gulf of their mutually unspoken yearnings.

Then T.C. reached out and turned on the ignition.
"Where are you going?" Tessa asked.

"I'm taking you back to your motel," he said
wearily. He looked at her once before pulling out
onto the road, but Tessa could not read his expression. He had pulled that careful veil of remoteness
back over his features, and she had no idea what he
was thinking.

She looked out her window in miserable silence
until T.C. pulled up in front of Tessa's motel room.
She sat still for a moment, then reached out her hand
for the door handle. But T.C. leaned across the car
and put his hand over hers, stopping her from opening the door.

"One thing I think you should know, Tessa," he

said. "You seem to have everything all figured out—
and it all looks pretty much like I'm the villain out to
rape the land, and Beryl's the poor old lady who's
about to lose her home. You've got us all neatly
pigeonholed—except for one thing. What about you,
Tessa Drew? Where do you fit into this unlovely
scheme? You've made it clear that you're working
with Beryl, but have you thought about why?"

Tessa blinked back new tears. His unexpected
assault frightened her—another example that she did
not know T.C. at all. It was all the more frightening
for its unerring accuracy. "I'm here...I'm here to do
a story," she managed to say.

"A story? Ah, so you're the objective reporter.
You're only doing your job, is that it? Is that the only
reason you're here?"

Tessa could see his jaw clench. *No, no!* she wanted
to cry out. *That's not the only reason! That's not the
reason at all!* But his eyes blazed out at her, and she
remembered that this was the man who was willing
to sell his friendship in the name of progress. She
could not bring herself to speak.

Now T.C. gave the door handle a swift shove, and
the door flew open. "I suggest you get some sleep,"
he said tightly. "You've got a busy day ahead of you,
I'm sure. And so do I."

She had no choice but to get out of the car in silence and watch helplessly as T.C. backed the car out
of the driveway, gunned the engine and drove away.
She could not see that he clenched the wheel in fury,
cursing his own stubbornness. For his plans had gone
seriously awry.

10

TESSA SPENT MOST OF THE NIGHT tossing and turning. She vacillated between being angry at T.C. for being so damned in control while she fell apart—attacking her when he knew he didn't have a leg to stand on—and being angry at herself for her incredible loss of control and her inability to counter his attack with the truth.

The truth was that she no longer knew what "the truth" meant. Her feelings for T.C. had come up on her so suddenly that she could barely focus on them. It was like trying to read a book that was held up to her nose. She had assumed that he felt something for her in return, but now, lying alone in her bed, she wondered if that was the case. And really, did she want to get involved with a man like T.C.—with any man, for that matter?

During the course of the night she managed to be angry, at one time or another, at everyone she knew. But as dawn crept under the shades of her boxlike motel room Tessa decided sheepishly that she had only herself to blame. If she had leveled with T.C.— if she had told him that she cared deeply for him, *but* that she needed to know how he felt about her, perhaps last night would not have happened. But the truth was, she had been unwilling to level with herself, so she could not possibly have done so with him.

Now, in the gray predawn light, she was able to regain some measure of sanity. She got out of bed before 6:00 A.M. and took a long hot shower to wash away what she now saw as the emotional excesses of the night before. The stinging water seemed to stir her sluggish powers of analysis back into operation, because by the time she had toweled dry Tessa had regained her perspective on the situation.

Of course, it was silly of her to have gotten so wrought up over what T.C. *didn't* say. Hadn't she been perfectly happy with things the way they were? And what did it matter how he was handling Beryl and her house? After all, he was only doing his job, and Tessa had always been the first to insist that people's jobs were only a part of their lives.

The thing to do was to go on and try to cancel out the turmoil of last night with a more rational attitude this morning. She would simply have to go back to Beryl's and get on with her job. T.C. would soon realize that she was not about to crumble under stress—that she, too, could separate her private from her public life. In fact, the harder she worked on the Beryl McGregor story, the more obvious it would be to him that she was willing to ignore what had happened between them last night. It was not just a matter of making the best of a bad situation. Tessa intended to do it up royally.

She spent an hour plotting out her strategy. It had become more important than ever that Beryl's cause be broadcast successfully far and wide. Tessa never did anything halfway, and now she had even more reason to make a big splash on Beryl's behalf. The cause had taken on a life of its own, fueled by last night's frustration and lack of communication.

The local broadcasts, Tessa decided, were not enough. Perhaps Beryl would do some speaking engagements. Perhaps a WBOS network affiliate would be interested in having Beryl appear on a national talk show. After all, the environmental issue was hot all over, and it would certainly gain Beryl some clout to appear on the "Today" show.

She packed a suitcase and was at Beryl's house before noon. She had no intention of interrupting her campaign for unimportant tasks like returning to the motel to eat and sleep. Beryl took one look at the suitcase and said, "There's a spare room at the top of the stairs."

Tessa spent all that day and the next calling local churches and clubs to see if they wanted Beryl McGregor or her representative to speak. On Monday morning she was on the phone to the network headquarters, offering them national coverage of the story as long as WBOS got to air the material first. She had not cleared this with Tim, but she figured he wouldn't mind as long as Channel 8 got first crack. She called a friend of hers on the staff of the *Boston Globe* and carefully orchestrated a telephone interview with Beryl—making sure that she only said things that had gone out over the WBOS broadcast over the weekend. Then she got to work on more broadcasts.

Beryl seemed to accept the flurry of activity around her in relative calm. She offered whatever information was requested and came across well in the *Boston Globe* interview, but she seemed more content to watch than participate. Several times Tessa had to search the grounds around the house to find Beryl rooting around in the garden or sitting by the trees, which offered the clear view of Choate I's crystal lake. But Tessa was so caught up in the momentum of the cause célèbre she had created, she never saw Beryl's tight smile as she stared out the windows of her living room to the ridge beyond the lake.

During those next few days Tessa neither saw nor heard from T.C. She thought about him often, of course, but not with anger or regret. She was doing something important too, she thought. She would show him that two could be busy being committed.

On Thursday morning a request came in to have Beryl McGregor speak at an emergency meeting of the Massachusetts Audubon Society. Tessa, who by then was taking all calls, put her hand over the mouthpiece and turned to Beryl, who was busy repotting a geranium on the kitchen table.

"Do we want to speak at the Mass. Audubon Society?" she whispered. "They're having an emergency meeting. I think it might be to try and raise some funds for you, Beryl. It could really help."

Beryl's back was to Tessa, but something in the way she laid down her trowel made Tessa start with surprise. When Beryl spoke, her voice was firm and controlled. "Do *we* want to speak at the Mass.

Audubon?" she asked. "No, Tessa, I don't think *we* want to do that. That is, you are perfectly able to go if you like. I would like to stay home—in my house."

This speech was at once chilling and perplexing. Tessa swallowed a sudden rise of fear in her throat. But she knew the people on the other end of the line were waiting. "Uh, I think we'll have to say no on this one," she said into the phone. "Things are getting kind of out of hand here, and Miss McGregor wants to stay close to home. Just in case—you know." She rang off with an apology and turned to Beryl. "What is it, Beryl?" she asked uneasily. "What's wrong?"

"I think you know what's wrong, Tessa. I'm glad to have you here with me, but you must see that you're going too far. You're being heavy-handed with *my* house—with *my* life—and I can't let you go on like that. I'm sorry." She shook her head, but her eyes were more sad than angry.

Tessa blinked. It suddenly occurred to her that their relationship had changed dramatically over the course of the week. She was no longer helping Beryl—she was running her life. She felt ashamed and was about to say so when the telephone rang again.

"Hello?" Tessa was aware of Beryl's steady gaze as she spoke.

"Tessa. It's Tim McNulty."

Just from the way he said his name, Tessa knew something was wrong. "Tessa," he said tersely, "you've got to stop. It's gone too far."

Tessa bit her lip and looked over at Beryl guiltily as if Beryl could hear what was being said. "What do you mean, Tim?" she inquired carefully.

"You know damn well what I mean." His voice was tense—not angry, but clearly upset. *Something's happened at the station*, she thought. "You're going too far in pushing this Beryl story. I got a call from network headquarters, and all the satellite affiliates are clamoring for more. You're overstepping your bounds, Tessa, and you know it. You had no authority to sell this story nationally!"

"Tim." She hoped her voice was low enough so that Beryl couldn't hear. "I'm just doing what I think is right. This is a big story, a great story—you said so yourself. I'm just making sure we get all the coverage we can. No one gets material that isn't directly attributable to us. Just think of the coverage we get out of this!"

"Tessa!" Now he was angry. "You're not covering this story—you're muckraking it. And it has to stop, now!"

"But Tim, this woman is about to lose her home! I've got to help her." She felt panic sweep over her in a great wave.

Tim sighed deeply. "Come back to Boston, Tessa. We have to talk."

"But Tim!"

"Come back. Now. This afternoon. Make your excuses and get back here. I expect you in my office at three sharp. Got it?"

Slowly she hung up the phone. The room was silent, but Tessa knew Beryl was waiting for her to speak. She suddenly wished that things between them had not changed—that Beryl was still the charming, independent woman who needed Tessa's support. Now, it seemed, it was the other way around.

"I have to go, Beryl," she said at last in a dull voice.

"What?" Beryl turned around slowly, but she did not seem surprised by the news. As a matter of fact, thought Tessa with a sinking heart, she looked relieved.

Tessa would not meet her eyes. "I have to go back to Boston. They want—they need me back at the station for something." Beryl was silent, and Tessa finally looked up at Beryl's face, now gentle with understanding.

"And I'm sorry—about everything!" Tessa suddenly blurted out. All at once she wanted to throw herself against Beryl's neck and seek her comforting arms. But she collected herself and forced a smile. "It's nothing important," she said brightly. "I'll probably be back tomorrow—you know how these things are. While I'm gone, make sure you sit tight and don't let anyone in who doesn't look right." Beryl smiled slightly at Tessa's effort to regain her former businesslike attitude.

"I'll be fine." Beryl assured her briskly. Then she led the way to the kitchen door. Tessa, suddenly at a loss for words, felt awkward and ill at ease.

"Well, I'd better hustle. I'll leave most of this stuff here, if that's okay with you."

"Fine," Beryl said again. She followed Tessa out into the yard. Tessa got into the car and sat for a moment to get her bearings. "Tessa?"

"Yes?" She looked out the window at the small woman framed by the old white house.

Beryl smiled an illuminating smile. "I'll see you soon, okay? And thanks for what you've done so far."

"Right." Tessa felt a great weight lifted off her shoulders. "See you soon." She grinned, waved and pulled away.

THE WEIGHT DESCENDED AGAIN as soon as she reached Boston. The very silence with which her entrance into the newsroom was greeted told Tessa that something was very wrong. And the look on Tim McNulty's face confirmed it.

"Sit down." He motioned to a chair across from his desk.

"Tim," she began, "I don't see what. . . ."

"Quiet!" He lifted his hand, and for the first time Tessa understood how upset he was. He was ordinarily an easygoing man. "Don't talk. Don't say a word. Just listen." He drew a deep breath. "Tessa, first of all I want you to understand this is not personal. This is not even my idea, but. . . ." He bit his lip, exasperated. "You went too far, Tessa. The station brass is going wild. They say you went over their heads in contacting the other stations, that you're conducting private business for the personal gain of your subject, that you've even accepted speaking engagements on her behalf. Is that true?"

"No!" Tessa sat up in her chair and then subsided.

"Well, the last part isn't true. I didn't accept any speaking engagements." In a smaller voice, she added, "Beryl didn't want to."

Tim nodded glumly. "But they're right about the rest. You went too far for this story, Tessa. I'm not sure what they're planning to do about it, but don't be surprised if you're reassigned."

"They can't!" Tessa was panicked, thinking of Beryl and the white house. "They can't do that to me—to her!" Tim was watching her in bleak silence. "It's just not fair, Tim," she murmured miserably.

"You're interfering with the news, Tessa. That's a cardinal sin in this business."

"That's not what you told me on Saturday," she snapped. "On Saturday, I was the golden girl around here. Everybody was falling all over themselves to help me out on this story. Fifteen phone calls on a Saturday night. Wasn't that some sort of record, Tim? Wasn't it?"

"That's not what's important," Tim said, sounding weary.

She stood up. "That's not what's important to you, you mean! You're sitting here in your snug little office while those people play God with the life of a wonderful woman!" She preferred not to think about the identity of "those" people. "You have no right to pull the rug out from under Beryl McGregor!"

"I'm not pulling the rug out from under her. I'm pulling it out from under you." Now Tim was angry as well. He looked at his watch and stood up. "Come on. The vice-president is waiting in the conference room with some MWC people who want to talk to you."

"Who?" For the first time she felt a stab of fear.

"Some state government people, I think. They're not very happy about all this, Tessa. We'd better let them tell you what they want to do."

Tessa felt doomed. She followed him out of his office and down the corridor, her heart in her throat. He was right. Things had gotten out of control. But she had never expected the station to abandon her. She was cold with apprehension.

As it turned out, the station was not ready to abandon her quite yet, for their own reasons. As a matter of fact, the government officials started out by applauding Tessa on the effectiveness of her reporting and on the commendable dedication it showed to her cause. Tessa was surprised that the government officials were doing most of the talking, not the station brass.

"It's not my cause," Tessa murmured dully. "It's Beryl McGregor's cause."

"Of course, of course," amended the official who smiled apologetically at her. "We understand. But you, Miss Drew, must understand that these things can get out of control. We fully support your right to represent Miss McGregor's point of view." This was said with such careful emphasis that Tessa knew a lawyer must be somewhere in the room. "All we are asking is that you refrain from extensive editorializing on the issue. You see, we feel that, whatever the outcome of this situation, in the long run, everybody will benefit from the results."

Tessa saw that Tim was as surprised as she was. But now she was only concerned with one thing.

"You mean I'm not off the story?" She looked from Tim to the station vice-president, who pursed his lips and shook his head. She could not tell what he was thinking.

"Of course you're not," the MWC official boomed. "We wouldn't think of pressuring the free press that way!" He laughed. "We just hope you go back out there and show our side of the story, too! Show how many people's lives will be enriched—maybe even saved by this new supply of fresh, clean water. Show how the people who were eager to sell feel about the Gemini Lakes." Tessa winced at the phrase but the man did not notice. "Show how much money we'll lose if there's another delay," he added with a bright chuckle, and everybody else in the room laughed as if on cue.

Tessa did not laugh. Money. That was at the root of the issue. And she knew that if she went back to Choate Hollow, she would have to play the game according to the money men. They were making the rules, free press notwithstanding. She felt drained of energy and emotion.

"Well, Tessa," Tim said in a low voice. "You've got another chance, it seems. What do you want to do with it?"

"I'll have to think about it," she said. She only wanted to get away from that smoke-filled room. She wanted to go home—not to Beryl's house, but to her own little apartment in the South End. She needed to be alone to think.

THE APARTMENT was just as she had left it. Had it really only been six days ago that she had set out for Choate

Hollow? Tessa threw herself onto the sofa in the living room and stared gloomily into the fireplace. The ashes from the fire T.C. had built were still lying in an unappetizing heap on the hearth. Tessa scowled and sniffled. Despite the warm June sunshine pouring into her bay window and the chirping of the grateful birds in the feeder, she felt as bleak as those ashes. Whatever had fired her up about Beryl McGregor's story had burned out in an afternoon. She no longer cared what happened.

The demoralizing conference at WBOS was not the only reason. There was also the nasty memory of the last time she had seen T.C. This reprimand—for she knew that insiders would eventually learn why she had been called up on the carpet at Channel 8— reinforced his position.

There was another reason for her low spirits. Shuffling through her accumulated mail when she got home, she had found a letter from Douglas. Well, it couldn't exactly be called a letter. It was typed on his Baltimore station's letterhead, and packed all the emotional impact of a form rejection slip.

"Apparently," she read, "you're still into playing cat and mouse with me. If you think I'm going to cool my heels down here while you take your sweet time about getting in touch with me, you've got another thought coming. You missed your chance. It's over. Douglas Bright."

Tessa could not believe it. The nerve of the guy, to assume she was just waiting for the right moment to get back in touch! Well, he'd never know that she had already—and very clearly—made up *her* mind never to see *him* again! In a fit of rage, she had torn the offending missive into tiny pieces and had crumbled it over the cold ashes, muttering curses under her breath. How like Douglas to insist on having the last word, even when there was no last word to give.

Tessa roamed restlessly around her three rooms for a while, put some classical music on her stereo and was just gearing herself up for a good bout of crying when her buzzer rang.

"Who is it?"

"It's Thomas Chimatsu."

The sound of his voice, unmistakable even through the metallic blur of the intercom, sent Tessa into a flurry of activity. She raced through her bedroom and into the bathroom to splash water on her face and check her eyes. On the way back she grabbed a red cotton pullover to replace the T-shirt she was wearing, and she paused on her way to the front door to kick a pile of clothing under the sofa.

T.C. found her panting with the sudden effort when he got upstairs. They looked at each other speculatively for a moment, and then he pulled his hands out from behind his back. He held out a huge bouquet of wild flowers, which he had obviously picked himself.

"Happy real birthday," he said in a soft, apologetic voice, and Tessa started to cry.

"Oh, Tessa." He stepped inside, dropped the flowers on a table and gathered her into his arms. Tessa was unable to protest, or to collect her thoughts enough to explain why she was in tears. She could only lean against him and weep.

"Shhhh." He stroked her head rhythmically, patiently, and didn't try to get her to stop. The mere fact that he was letting her cry calmed her down somewhat, so that in a few moments the sobs had subdued to occasional hiccups. "Now," he said, "tell me what's going on around here."

She nodded and took a deep breath. "They don't want me to continue with the story. They're afraid I might cost the MWC too much money. They told me I was losing my objectivity. And then, when I got home, I got this awful letter from Douglas." She had forgotten that he knew nothing of Douglas, but he merely nodded his head and let her go on. "And it really made me feel helpless and mad, and then... and then...I even forgot that today was my real birthday!"

This last was sounded on a wail of renewed tears. She was about to lay her head back against his chest, but he picked up her chin between his thumb and forefinger and studied her face. "Come on," he said briskly. "You need to get out of here. A nice walk will do you good.... Yes, it will...come on now...." And he maneuvered her bodily out of the apartment and down the stairs.

They walked across town to the Charles River esplanade. It was late afternoon, and the shaded paths were filled with sunbathers and afternoon athletes and children rolling on the green. Across the river, the MIT campus shimmered in stately beauty. The willows along the banks of the river dipped gracefully to the water's edge.

As they walked, Tessa told him everything that

had happened since she had seen him last on Saturday night. She told him about all the efforts she had made to get Beryl's story to the public, and exactly what the reactions had been. She described each development in great detail, as if she were recalling the events in her own mind in order to clarify them. She told him what had happened at the station that afternoon—what the station management had said, and what the MWC officials had said.

And she told him how Beryl had reacted—how she, Tessa, had felt that Beryl was somehow remote from all the effort she was making, and how odd that made her feel. She told him that she didn't even understand it herself, but that she had been sure she was doing the right thing.

It was as if a dam had burst inside her. Once she started confessing her doubts, confusions and convictions, she could not stop. She told him about Douglas. T.C. listened, nodding occasionally and once in a while asking a question. But mostly he was silent, absorbing her tremendous outpouring of words without protest.

Tessa hardly thought about what she was saying. It seemed that she had been alone with her doubts for too long—for years, perhaps, since she had never talked to Douglas this way. She felt strangely detached from the dark-haired woman who strode alongside of the handsome man, urgently pouring out her heart and mind. She could not stop.

By the time she finally wound down, it was dusk, and they had followed the riverside path all the way down to the Harvard Business School, where the low-slung bridges across to Cambridge were reflected along with the tall brick buildings of the school in the mist-colored river.

"I don't know why I'm telling you all this," she said, narrowing her eyes so that the traffic streaming by on the other shore became a blur of red and white lights. "I feel so silly, babbling on about things that don't concern you." She looked sideways at his profile. The only thing she had not spoken of was her feelings for him. She wondered if he had missed that in her monologue.

"It's not a question of it concerning me," he said. "If you want to talk about something, then that concerns me."

She felt a stab of bitterness. "But you don't get so caught up in things. You manage to stay . . . above it all."

He gave her a swift, speculative glance. "Not above it all," he corrected. "I'm certainly not above it all." He turned back to the river. "I just approach things differently than you."

"How do you approach them, T.C.?"

"More cautiously, for one thing. I've always felt the need to separate my work from my personal life. It's a sort of separate-but-equal policy that I've developed over the years. That's why when I'm with you I really try not to think about the Gemini Lakes." He paused. "And vice versa."

Tessa could not keep the bitterness from her voice. "Unless I make it impossible for you to ignore, is that it, T.C.?"

He smiled patiently. "I wish you wouldn't take it

so personally. It's not you—it's not me. We all stand
to gain from the Gemini Lakes." He looked at Tessa
and sighed heavily. "Yes, even Beryl." He shook his
head. "It's important not to lose sight of the forest for
the trees. At least, it's important to me."

"And that's what you think I do. Lose sight of the
forest."

"Yes, you do. In this case, I think you do."

Now it was Tessa's turn to laugh. "You know, it's
funny. I always used to be the one who had the perspective. I was always the one who held back, the
one who had the whole picture under control." She
turned to him. "I don't know what's happening to
me," she added bleakly.

Thomas was silent. For a moment she thought he
had not even heard her, so absorbed was he in his
own thoughts. But then he looked at her searchingly,
and she met his gaze, willing him to say something
that would help.

Twice he opened his mouth to speak, and twice he
shut his lips firmly again as if to keep the words from
escaping without his permission. When at last he did
speak, Tessa knew he was not saying what he had
planned to say.

"I've never been a believer in astrology," he
mused, "but I guess there's something to it. I mean,
you and I are a lot alike in many ways...." He shook
his head when he saw that she was about to protest.
"No, not in the obvious ways. I mean, of course,
we're different too, but there may be something to
this Gemini bit. To be living so completely in your
head, in your intellect, to always be seeing both sides

of the issue...." His eyes narrowed and he shook his head. "It's not always a blessing, you know."

"But I don't. I don't see both sides of this issue." Tessa's voice was full of wonder, since what she was thinking was a revelation to herself. "It's as if I got myself so totally absorbed in this thing that I can't see to the other side—and yet, I don't know how I came to be so involved in the first place. God knows I am not a rabid environmentalist."

He looked at her sideways. "Meaning I am, I suppose."

Tessa flushed. "I mean you *should* be committed to Beryl's cause, to saving that natural environment the way it is, more than I should be. The way you talked about the recreational use of the preserve around Choate I—how can you worry about the eagles and not about a human being?"

"Because the eagles can't advocate for themselves and Beryl can. Because Beryl has you and they don't. Because Beryl can sit in her beloved house and find herself on national television."

Tessa absorbed the meaning of this with difficulty. "Is that why you brought Beryl and me together? To even out the balance of power?" She was incredulous, although she knew she should not have been. T.C. nodded, and Tessa winced in pain. "She used me, then. You used me, too." When T.C. did not respond, but continued to look at her in compelling silence, Tessa went on. "Yes, yes, I know. I used her as well. And you. I know." She felt tears bubbling up beneath her eyelids, but she managed to blink them down. "What I don't understand is how it came to this—where did my point of view change?"

"Maybe," T.C. said gently, "maybe it means you're starting to care."

Tessa was stunned by this statement. "What do you mean?" she stammered. Was he finally going to say something to her—something about *them*?

T.C.'s eyes searched her face, but his voice did not betray him. "I mean, maybe you're learning that some things are important to you, Tessa Drew, no matter what situation you find yourself in. Some things are unchangeable once they happen, even to the ever-mutable Gemini twins."

She thought she detected a melancholy note in his voice. "Do you mean, like the Gemini Lakes?" she asked him.

He smiled. "Yes, like the Gemini Lakes. Among other things."

Tessa leaned back on the grass and turned her gaze out to the river. She did not want those eyes on hers while she spoke. She didn't trust herself to speak carefully if they were. Her feelings might come forth in a foolish rush if they were. So she averted her head. "Do you mean," she asked slowly, "that I have to learn to be committed to something? Is that what you think?"

"I do. I think you have to decide what's important to you, Tessa, and never let yourself be persuaded otherwise. You may think I'm remote and detached sometimes—" he put his hand out as she looked up at him sharply "—no, I know you do. But I try to live my life by some principles that are important to me. I

try to be consistent in my beliefs." Now it was T.C.
who turned away from Tessa's gaze. "Although
sometimes it's hard to stick to your own program."
He turned back and took one of her hands in his.
"Sometimes, even the best-laid plans have to give
way to new realities."

Tessa began to understand what T.C. was trying
to say although she could not understand why he did
not just come right out and say it. He, too, had a set
of realities by which he lived. His involvement with
the Gemini Lakes project was part of that. And his
involvement with her was something he still struggled with, just as she had struggled with it in the beginning. If she wanted T.C.—if she wanted anything
in her life—she would have to fight for it.

And that meant fighting for the other things that
were important to her as well. It meant going back to
Choate Hollow and helping Beryl try to save her
house. Not to save it for her, but to be there to help.
Her heart *was* committed to Beryl McGregor, just as
T.C. was committed to the Gemini Lakes. And after
that, after they had both proved to themselves that
they did have the courage of their convictions, then
perhaps they would have the courage to assess their
future together.

She felt filled with a secret exultation. For a long
time she had truly doubted her ability to be totally
committed to something. Now she knew that she
could. Rather than feeling trapped by this revelation,
she felt a great sense of freedom. She felt as if something tight—a spring, perhaps, or a knot—had been
uncoiled with a sudden release of pressure. She could

care about something. And if she could care, she could also love.

But Tessa knew that now was not the time to declare as much to T.C. She would have to honor his reserve for as long as he needed it. The only thing to do now was to wait. If there was one thing she had learned from T.C. and Beryl, she thought ironically, it was patience.

She turned to T.C., who had been watching her with a bemused smile on his face. "Well, Miss Drew," he said, "it appears that that overactive mind of yours has been doing some heavy thinking."

"You could hear the wheels clanking, huh?"

"And the steam rising and everything. Care to share your conclusions with me?" For an instant, Tessa thought she saw an expression of intense longing cross his features. But then he chucked her under the chin and grinned, erasing the moment. "What have you decided to do about Beryl McGregor?"

Tessa smiled. She knew that he sensed what she had been thinking, and that he had deliberately steered the conversation back to Beryl. But that was all right. She could wait. "As if you didn't know exactly what I'm going to do. Go back to Choate Hollow, of course. I wouldn't dream of missing the next installment of this story."

They exchanged knowing glances of approval and understanding. "But tonight," she went on, standing up and stretching out her hand for T.C.'s, "tonight I intend to celebrate with a vengeance. After all, this is my real birthday. And besides, I deserve it."

They got up and started walking, hand in hand,

back to the path. "By the way," she said, "I never found out when your real birthday is. When is it?"

He turned and, smiling, placed a kiss on the tip of her nose. "Happy real birthday," he said. "To both of us."

11

THEY WALKED across the Weeks footbridge and along the Cambridge bank of the river to Harvard Square. The streets were full of evening strollers, many of whom gathered in the little plazas and parks that dotted the square to watch the street performers. Jugglers, mimes, acrobats and musicians of every persuasion could be seen in every available open space and storefront, performing for the crowd and for the coins and bills that were tossed into receptacles at their feet. A jazz trumpet solo mingled with a woodwind duet, which vied with a jug band, all punctuated by the laughter of a crowd watching four clowns juggle fruit.

Tessa felt as if it was a party being thrown especially for her, even though she knew that the scene was a common one on warm nights all summer long. She and T.C. decided against dinner and opted instead for a visit to a local ice-cream parlor where, amid old oak paneling and marble-topped counters, they both ordered hot-fudge sundaes with all the trimmings. The store was already selling Fourth of July treats and favors, and T.C. purchased a sparkler like the one that had graced their baked Alaska dessert at the Ritz. Solemnly, he placed it on top of Tessa's gooey mountain of hot fudge and mocha nut ice cream, and they watched it burn down to the thin metal stub before diving into the sticky sweets themselves. Tessa vowed that she had not had so much fun since her parents had taken her with six friends to a make-your-own-sundae emporium for her tenth birthday.

Then T.C. took her to a basement coffee house to hear folk music. He told Tessa that he had frequented the tiny cellar shop many times as a college student and that the particular guitar and banjo duo they were about to hear had been one of his favorites. They ordered huge mugs of tart apple cider to offset the sundaes and waited for the music to begin.

Tessa had never been much of a folk-music fan, but it intrigued her to think of T.C. as an idealistic college student, nursing a mug of hot mulled cider while pondering the harmonic lyrics of the musicians on the postage-stamp stage. Tonight, when everything seemed touched by the gentle glow of new-found satisfaction, she was able to listen to the twangy melodies with a new ear, and imagined herself as T.C.'s collegiate date for the evening, sitting close together on the uncomfortable chairs and thinking the future was theirs.

In a way, it was. Tessa felt a tremendous sense of liberation from the tensions that had been haunting her all day and the doubts that had been plaguing her for the past week. She no longer felt guilty about her motives for becoming involved with Beryl McGregor. The fact that she *was* involved, totally, was good enough for her. What happened now, was not as important as the fact that she had taken that step.

She turned and looked at T.C., who was absorbed in the music and his own private reveries of the past. In the dim light of the candles that burned on their table, his face looked very young, and it was easy to indulge in her fantasy of T.C. as a college romance. He looked so innocent, so idealistic, as he nodded his head slightly in time to the music.

And yet, this was the man who had refused to admit that his involvement with the Gemini Lakes was partly responsible for Beryl McGregor losing her home. The man who had insisted that his private views had nothing to do with his work—and that his relationship with Tessa had nothing to do with either.

Some things, thought Tessa dreamily, *are unchangeable. But others can change.* T.C. may once have been an idealist. Now he was something different—Tessa was not sure what.

Better not to deal with that right now, she reminded herself. First, she had to bring her story at Choate Hollow to a conclusion. Then she could deal with her feelings about T.C. Douglas had been right about one thing: Tessa was very good at postponing her emotions. But deny them? Not her!

Right now she wanted only one thing. Two things, really. "T.C.," she whispered, putting her hand on his arm to get his attention.

"Hmm?" He seemed to come back to reality with a start.

"Will you promise me something?"

He smiled. "A birthday promise?"

"Yes, you could call it that. I told you I wouldn't

take extraordinary measures to help Beryl keep her house. I want you to promise that you won't try and get her to change her mind. You have a lot of influence over her, you know."

T.C. searched her face in the candlelight and nodded. "It's a deal. I won't try to get her to do what she doesn't want to do." He met her gaze steadily, and Tessa wondered why he seemed to hesitate before answering. But then he smiled and reached for her hand.

"Now I want you to promise me something in return," he said.

"What?"

"Promise me we can go home together as soon as this set is over and make love all night long."

That was the other thing she had wanted.

"GOD, TESSA! I need you so badly! I want you so much!"

T.C.'s voice, ragged and torn with passion, reached Tessa through a muffled veil of sensation. It was hours since they had spilled onto her bed together, and the time had been warped by the overwhelming need to speak to each other in the language they both seemed to share.

"Come inside me, T.C. Now. I want you now." They had made love many times—more times than Tessa could count. But somehow, exhaustion had not dimmed their mutual desire, and each orgasm seemed to bring them closer to the edge of that commitment that neither of them could make in words. Now Tessa, who had promised not to, found herself biting her lips to keep herself from crying out "I love you!" as T.C.

entered her yet again, his maleness cloaked in velvet at first, then unleashed as Tessa's warm loins urged him deeper. For the first time in all their lovemaking, she could feel him shudder and slowly lose that masterly control. Above her, his face paled, then flushed. His eyes opened wide, as if he were seeing something he had not seen before. Then they closed tightly against the rushing tide that enveloped him with a wrenching groan. His slow, exquisitely orchestrated pace quickened into a frenzied rhythm that seemed to beat at the very door of Tessa's soul. In a way, this T.C. was a stranger to her, and frightening in his intensity. But Tessa, as she rode with him to heights of ecstasy she could barely endure, was aware of a stunning shock of recognition. This, she felt, was the T.C. she had been waiting to meet. This was a man committed—in body, if nothing else.

Then, what she thought had been the pinnacle of sensation became only the halfway point, and she could no longer think clearly

THEY DIDN'T MAKE LOVE all night long. At least Tessa was not aware of the dawn light creeping in under her window shades when at last she sank into an exhausted sleep. She lay with her body stretched cattycorner across her bed, anchoring T.C.'s limbs down beneath her in an abandonment of physical possession. If nothing else, they had possessed each other in that way by now. Their knowledge of each other's bodies, of their threshold for passion and their limit for release, was complete and exhaustive. And exhausting. In that misty moment before sleep, Tessa wondered if she had ever been so completely filled and satiated by another person in her life. Certainly not in the physical sense, for lovemaking with Douglas had been almost competitive in nature, and before him her love life had been sporadic at best.

With T.C. it was different. She was so totally absorbed by the experience of exploring his body and of opening hers up for his exploration, that she felt she had been loved right through to the core of her soul. Every limb, every nook and cranny had been paid homage to, and she found herself without shame in the pursuit of homage to his. Together, they were compelled to seek greater heights of sensation and possession, and now, in the dim shadows of the darkened room, she felt filled up with him—with his touch, with his smell, with his very breath. She drifted into the sleep of the well content.

T.C. lay awake, very still beneath the light burden of Tessa's limbs thrown across his own. He stared up at the high ceiling as if he could read a message on the blank dark surface. If Tessa had been awake, she would not have noticed anything unusual about the placid composure of his features. But T.C. was very good at keeping his deepest thoughts well hidden in the private recesses of his mind. And deep down, he was anything but composed. The events of the past few weeks had agitated him almost as much as they had agitated Tessa. At first he had not recognized this fact, but the feelings had accumulated and accelerated until tonight, when he had realized the extent of his inner turmoil.

All his life, T.C. had lived by carefully arranged

precepts. His schooling followed one well-planned course, his career another. Even his love life had taken a clear and careful path. But shortly before meeting Tessa, he had suddenly become involved with someone and veered from that path. After a brief, but traumatic relationship, he had picked up the threads of his life, but had vowed that such erratic behavior would never happen again.

Now, his mind raced back and forth from the past to the future. He turned his head to the woman sleeping beside him. What did the future hold for her—for them? The light covers in which they had been wrapped had been completely discarded during their furious hours of lovemaking, and now he dared not disturb her by reaching down to pick them up. Her body lay exposed to him in the silver half-light of predawn. The breasts, small but full and superbly shaped, he thought, rose and fell with the steady rhythm of her breathing. Her ribs appeared to tremble slightly with each breath, and it gave her torso an appearance of frailty that he knew was deceiving. She was strong and agile, and he had never had an experience like he had with her in bed. He felt his passion stirring and willed himself back into composure.

Her face, seen in profile, looked so open and lovely that he ached with tenderness. The profile was like his own, he knew, but only to the discerning eye. Her nose was thinner, her mouth gentler, and her chin tilted up at the tip. Her eyes, he knew, were more full of gold fire than his, which were more like green water. Curious, he thought, with a small smile—the two air signs, and both so full of fire and water. The ever-mutable twins.

She had come into his life and made more difference than he dared admit, to himself or to her. He was being forced to question what he had long ago hoped to put to rest—his own convictions about life and work and commitment. Part of him resented having been put on the spot like this again, even if Tessa could not possibly be held responsible. And part of him could not stay away from her vibrant energy, her insatiable curiosity about life, about him.

Still, he knew what he had to do. He owed it to himself to continue acting as he always had, according to a strict set of guidelines that he had mapped out long ago. Self-discipline was a challenge to him, and he accepted its necessity now without question— or at least, without allowing himself to stick around for the answers.

Slowly, in a series of tiny movements that took over twenty minutes, he extricated himself from beneath her slumberous limbs. Once standing, he stood naked before her for another long while, staring down at her sleeping face, wondering what she was dreaming to put such an expression of childish repose on her features. He hoped it was about him. Then he tiptoed out of the room, dressed quickly in the bathroom and let himself out of the apartment without making a sound.

TESSA'S FIRST THOUGHT on waking was that he had not been there at all, that it had all been a strange and wonderfully erotic dream. How, she pondered sleepily, could he possibly have extricated himself from the knot of limbs they had made last night? Then she became aware of a dull, not unpleasant ache in her thighs, and she smiled. He had been and gone.

But where? And when? Surely there was no reason for him not to spend the entire night in her bed. He had done it before, and she in his. She tried to think back to that half-remembered moment before she had fallen asleep. Had he mentioned something to her about having to leave? Had he left her then? No, she clearly recalled that he had been lying beside her, warm and fragrant, as her eyes fell shut. And she recalled that they had long been beyond normal modes of conversation by that time. They had spoken with their bodies, and their mouths had used no spoken words to communicate the most subtle messages.

His leaving had not been one of those messages. But Tessa, blinking herself out of sleep and into the bright morning sunshine that filled the room, decided that if he had left it had been for a very good reason.

She got up, stretched and growled lazily and went into the bathroom to shower and dress. It was there she saw the note. "Have to go to New York this afternoon, and need to make a few stops first. Couldn't bear to wake you, Sleeping Beauty. Could hardly bear to go. Soon. T.C."

It was not a particularly illuminating note, but Tessa, still full of the romance of their night together, was not fazed by its brevity. She was more confident than ever before that sooner or later she and T.C. would be able to make a commitment to each other. The fact that she would rather it be sooner than later was just something she would have to live with, patiently. And, of course, having nights like the one they had just shared would make the waiting a lot easier. Tessa looked at the message taped to the mirror, leaned forward and planted a warm kiss on the paper. Then she stared at herself in the mirror for as long as she could without breaking into a smile. Yes, she decided, there was no doubt about it. This was a happy person.

It seemed that her life had fallen together with remarkable ease, considering the state she had been in twenty-four hours ago. She felt a remarkable clarity of purpose, and she was determined not to lose sight of it. She called Tim McNulty and let him know that she had decided to continue on with the story, and that she was willing to keep within the bounds of journalistic objectivity. She offered no apologies, and he seemed to want none. "Get back out there, Tessa," he said, and Tessa knew he was glad she had decided to stick with it.

She drove out to Choate Hollow in a rented car, idly flipping the dial on the AM radio to get the news on all the stations. She felt as if she had been out of touch with the rest of the world for the past week, as if the entire universe had been telescoped into a twelve-mile-square parcel of land known as Choate Hollow. Or the Gemini Lakes.

Just as she pulled off the highway, she heard one of the news announcers say, ". . . from Choate Hollow." She turned the radio up. "District courts today have said that they are willing to grant an additional postponement to Miss Beryl McGregor, of the tiny hamlet that is scheduled to go under ninety feet of water in the state's huge reservoir project, the Gemini Lakes. Miss McGregor is the last of the homeowners to leave the area and the only one to raise any resistance to the project, which is being held up while the matter is decided by the courts. This morning's ruling means an extra week for Miss McGregor, whose cause has been given much media attention, thanks to the efforts of Channel 8's Focus Team reporter Tessa Drew. The extension on the delay was granted, according to court officials, due to Miss McGregor's age and the popularity of her cause, even though it means thousands of dollars in additional construction costs."

Tessa let out a whoop that reverberated in the small car. An extra week! And Tessa had been safely in Boston, unable to exert undue influence. Now *that* was news! And who knew? It just might be possible that a deal could be worked out with the MWC—after all, *they* were the ones on the defensive now— whereby the McGregor house could be preserved, or at least moved to another location. Despite all the work Tessa had been doing to bring Beryl's plight to public attention, this option had never really occurred to her, and now it filled her with a delicious sense of anticipation. She had never expected this story—or her involvement in Beryl's cause—to go this far. Beryl might actually win!

She drove straight up to Beryl's house, envisioning a triumphant return to a triumphant scene. Instead, she found Beryl standing in the front yard, looking as if she had been waiting for Tessa for some time.

"Beryl! I just heard about the second delay! Congratulations!"

Beryl smiled, but there was something about her face that chilled Tessa's high spirits. "You must be so excited," Tessa went on, hoping she was mistaken. "It looks like you might have a fighting chance now!"

"Looks that way." Beryl turned and led the way—not into the house but around it, to the woods that sloped down by the lake. "How was Boston?" she asked as they picked their way over the pine-carpeted earth.

"Boston was fine." Tessa knew by now that something was wrong—very wrong. Beryl should be delighted, but she was not. "Where are we going?" she asked.

"You'll see." Beryl smiled encouragingly at Tessa, but Tessa did not smile back. As if aware she had made her young friend nervous, Beryl launched into a rambling account of her years spent as a student nurse in Boston.

But Tessa, with her newswoman's instincts, was not fooled. She knew Beryl had something to tell her—something far more important than an account of the poor working conditions in Boston hospitals fifty years ago. One thing Beryl had never done was dwell on the past. She had always seemed to be much more concerned with the present—and the future. Now she droned on and on recalling tiny details of her life back then, and commenting on how much it had changed. But Tessa knew she could not stop Beryl. She could only wait. Whatever Beryl had to say, she was obviously going to take her time to say it.

The woods rose up in sheer walls of green on either side of the narrow road down which they traveled. The sunlight flashed and danced through the branches in a blinding game of hide and seek. Suddenly it all seemed ominous, especially since Tessa sensed that Beryl was as nervous as she was.

They walked in silence for a few moments, and then Beryl veered off the narrow path and seemed to disappear into a thicket of bushes. Tessa took a deep breath and followed. There was a low tunnel through the brush that led, after a moment, into a small clearing. Tessa straightened up. They were at the edge of Choate I. She turned around, and saw that they had not gone very far from the house, although it was all but obscured through the thick undergrowth. All she could see of it was the steep pitch of the gabled roof.

Beryl had plunked herself down on a patch of dry grass and positioned herself to gaze out over the water. Tessa followed her lead. On this silent, sun-drenched day, the lake had an almost prehistoric clarity to it. It was hard to believe that Choate I was man-made, so superbly did it fit into Tessa's image of classic virgin wilderness.

Beryl turned and saw Tessa's tensed pose, and she reached out to pat her hand. "See that island out there, Tessa—that little puff of land? That used to be a mountain."

"A mountain? Out here?" Tessa tried to look interested.

"Well," chuckled Beryl, "that was long before my time, of course. Time wore 'em down to hills by the time I came along. But boy, they were rugged hills.

And out over there, to the south...see that little spit of land rising up from the shore. Well, down there, that's where...."

Tessa could stand the suspense no longer. "Beryl. Please, stop." Beryl broke off as if surprised by Tessa's vehemence.

"What is it, honey?"

"I want you to tell me what's happening. Why are you telling me all this?"

Beryl cocked her head to one side, her face in a half smile. "Why, I thought you wanted to hear about this kind of thing. For the story, I mean."

Tessa ignored the attempt to draw her off the subject. "You've got something on your mind, Beryl, and I want to know what it is. Does it have to do with that second extension you got this morning? I heard about that on the radio coming out. Please, tell me," she finished beseechingly.

Beryl nodded. "It has nothing to do with that second extension, Tessa. *I* had nothing to do with that. My lawyers got that without even consulting me. It wasn't my doing at all."

Tessa stared at her. "But aren't you glad you got it? I mean, it looks like maybe you've got a fighting chance after all. Maybe you can save the house, get it moved...or you can even—" Tessa broke off when she saw that Beryl was sadly shaking her head.

"I'm sorry," was all Beryl said, but Tessa already understood that Beryl had changed her mind about saving the house. She was not going to fight anymore.

Tessa tried to think of something to say, but she

could not, nor would she have been capable of
speech if she had. All she could do was stare at Beryl,
who smiled back at her with that bittersweet expression, shaking her head sympathetically, as if it was
Tessa who needed the comfort, not her. And it was
true. Tessa put her fingers to her cheeks and felt the
surprising dampness of tears. She was weeping,
quietly, helplessly, without quite knowing why.

"Tessa," said Beryl gently, "listen to me. I want
you to look out there again. No, over there, over to
the south, to that tip of land. See it? That used to be
the most beautiful wooded knoll. There were trees
forty to fifty feet high up there—mighty pines and
oaks. Do you believe it? And my friends...I told
you about the Swensons, didn't I? Well, the Swensons had a spread on that knoll that looked like it
was the model for an English picture postcard. Nobody in the valley knew how old man Swenson got
his land to look so gently green and fertile. Blue ribbon farming, that's what they used to call it in the
valley."

Tessa was totally caught up in the picture Beryl
was painting with her delicate words and gestures,
and she had calmed down somewhat. "It must have
been so beautiful," she whispered. "So very beautiful."

"It was, Tessa. The most beautiful place in the
world to me. But you know something? It's beautiful
now, too. Look! Look at the way the sun shines off
the water, making a mirror along the peninsula there!
Look at the way the trees fill the horizon, dancing
around the lake like that in the wind. Isn't that love-

ly?" For the first time, her voice cracked. She was silent for a moment, but her expression, when she finally turned back to Tessa, was sweet and clear.

"You see, Tessa, I hold two beauties in my mind. One of the past, and one of the present. They're both beautiful, and I'm glad I have them both. Someday, maybe you'll be able to do that, too. It's just a matter of perspective."

A matter of perspective. Suddenly, a light bulb lit up in Tessa's brain. That thought—a matter of perspective—reminded her of someone else. And then, with a terrible clarity, she understood what must have happened.

"Beryl, did T.C. come out here this morning to see you by any chance?"

"Why, yes he did." Beryl looked surprised. "He was on his way to New York or someplace, and just stopped in to say good morning. How did you know?"

Tessa had to grip her fists tightly together to control the sudden wave of anger that threatened to envelop her. "A lucky guess," she muttered bitterly.

"He said he was just checking in to see how I was doing. He was here when I got the news about the second extension, as a matter of fact." She looked at Tessa sharply. "He wanted to talk about something else this morning," she said.

"I'll bet he did." Tessa was seething. He had promised not to interfere with Beryl, and he had betrayed that promise.

"When we are together," she remembered him saying once, "then you are all the world to me. But when

I am at work, that is my world." Well, he had been at work this morning, and who knew? Perhaps last night, too, had been part of his job.

"He promised," she whispered desolately.

"What?" Beryl looked concerned. "Tessa, what's wrong?"

Tessa took Beryl's hands in hers. "Beryl, listen to me. You can't listen to what T.C. tells you. He's poisoned your mind."

"What are you talking about?"

"This morning, when he came to see you. He came to talk you out of staying here, don't you see? He has only to gain by convincing you of all this claptrap about two beauties, and about keeping one's perspective. Beryl, it's *your* home, not his!"

Beryl shook her head and withdrew her hand. "He didn't come here to poison my mind, honey. As a matter of fact, he opened it. This hasn't been my home for years. Not since Choate I, and maybe not even before then. I had left Choate Hollow long ago, and I've always made it a policy not to look back." She stood up and reached out her hand to help Tessa to her feet. "In any case," she added gently, "T.C. said nothing to me about all of that this morning. I've been thinking about giving in for a while, and he's known it. We've had many discussions. But this morning was not one of them. Believe me, he had other things on his mind."

Tessa did not know whether to believe Beryl or not. She stood up and began following Beryl back through the underbrush toward the house. "If that's true," she said, trying not to sound accusing, "why did you hold out this long? Why did you try to stop them in the first place?"

Beryl shrugged. "For old times' sake, I guess—the melancholy instincts of an old woman. I thought I owed it to myself, to my past. And I felt a little guilty about not having real strong ties, like everybody figured I should. But then I began to realize that I'm not a melancholy old woman. Hell, I'm not even that old, by McGregor standards! Seventy-two—I could have years of life left in me! Who knows what adventures lie ahead?" She turned in the kitchen doorway and looked back over the path they had just taken. The silver wedge of lake was just visible through the greenery. "I needed to take that stand for a while, I guess," she said softly. "It was the only way I could think of to say goodbye."

"But you might have been able to save the house! You might not have had to say goodbye!" All the pain of Tessa's betrayal seeped into her voice. "You might have won, don't you see?"

Beryl looked at her sympathetically. "I have won, though, Tessa. I have what I want—my past and my future. Doesn't that sound good to you?" She watched as Tessa's face once again crumpled into tears, and then reached out to draw her into the house with her. "If it's T.C. you're worried about...."

"I'm not worried about T.C.!"

"If it's T.C. you're angry with, then...." Beryl ignored Tessa's statement. "You must believe me. He did not betray me. And he most certainly did not betray you, Tessa."

Tessa looked at Beryl and saw that this was true. Neither T.C. nor Beryl was capable of subterfuge.

Beryl led Tessa to the kitchen table, still holding her hand as if she were a child. "Come and sit down," she said. "Tessa, I'm sorry about all this. You've been a wonderful help to me, more than I can tell you. Your energy, your dedication, your commitment—" She broke off and looked at her closely. "Don't ever lose that. You're part of what made me see that I want to go on, and I thank you for that. But this is what I want to go on to. We all have to decide what it is we really want, don't we?"

Tessa couldn't answer. She felt absolutely powerless. Now she had nothing to fight for. All she wanted to do was to go away somewhere and lick her wounds.

Quietly, Beryl got up and went to the cabinet, from which she produced two glasses and a bottle of homemade wine. She brought these back to the table and poured a full glass for both of them. Tessa took hers and drank listlessly. "T.C. is coming back tonight," Beryl said conversationally. "He said to ask you to wait here, if you like." When Tessa did not reply, Beryl moved on to other subjects. "You know, I'm going to get a pretty penny for this place, Tessa. When they heard about the second extension, Commissioner Conklin and his cronies called to quote me an absurdly high price." She chuckled. "Really absurd."

"Are you going to take it?" Somehow, the image of Beryl as being money hungry had never occurred to Tessa.

"Are you kidding? Of course I am. This is now prime real estate, and worth every penny. Your publicity helped see to that, you know. Anyway, with prices like this, I'm going to need that money to put a down payment on another house. I think I'll move closer in to the city. Maybe even right into town—who knows?"

Tessa knew Beryl was trying to be gay for her benefit, but the most she could manage in reply was a weak smile. She was still too absorbed by her own private failure.

"I want you here when I tell Commissioner Conklin I'll take his money and he can have my house," Beryl told her. "I intend to wait until the bulldozers are chomping at my door—right before my deadline is up." She put down her wineglass and peered at Tessa. "You will be here, won't you?"

Tessa shook her head. "I don't know, Beryl."

"Will you be here tonight, when T.C. gets back?"

"I don't know that, either." And she truly did not know. But there was something she felt had to be said. "Beryl, I just want you to know something. When I decided to take on your story...when I first agreed to help you out...it wasn't because I really believed in your cause. I did it because I had to prove something to myself. I used you for that, and I want to apologize."

"Oh, honey. Come on, don't put yourself through this. I used you, too, don't you see that? We all did what we could for our own reasons. And now, we all have to act on our own consciences. As long as we truly believed in what we were doing at the time, then what we did was right. The important thing is . . . no regrets."

Tessa felt tears welling up in her eyes again. No regrets? Ah, that was not so easy. "That's just it," she said. "All I'm left with are regrets."

"Tessa. I said, no regrets. And you have to trust me on this one, because . . . well, because I know better." Tessa looked up, clearly unconvinced. "Believe me, you have more than you know you have—you just have to be willing to recognize it. My money's on you." She paused, as if debating whether to go on. "And my money's on T.C., too." Tessa started to protest that T.C. had nothing to do with it, but Beryl scolded her into silence. "Don't argue with me, young lady. I'm talking to you! Thomas Chimatsu is the most dedicated man I know. And when he decides on a course of action, you just try and change his mind."

"But people do," Tessa said. "They do change their minds. Look at you."

Beryl shook her head. "No, I never really did. I mean, this, now, feels right to me, like staying and fighting never did. And besides," she added softly, "if you really love someone, you take those chances. That's what loving is all about."

Tessa took another sip of wine, but she still had trouble controlling her voice. "I'm scared, Beryl," she whispered.

Beryl came around to her side of the table and slipped into the chair next to her. She reached out and drew her close into a warm hug. "I know, honey. I know. I was scared, too, at first. And you know what? I think your friend is, too."

"T.C.?" It was hard for Tessa to imagine him afraid.

"T.C. And I think one of you better figure something out before both of you lose. There will be no winners in this game if you don't speak up for what you want. Now finish your wine."

Tessa did so and then followed Beryl out to the car. She got into the driver's side, and Beryl leaned her head in after. "I'll tell you what. I won't let anyone else know about my decision until Monday. I can pack things up on the sly so I'll be ready to get out quick when Conklin comes around. That gives you four days to decide what you want to do about seeing this story through to the finish. And about various other things, of course. If you want to see this through to its logical conclusion, I'd welcome it, Tessa. It would make me happy to share this little victory with you. But if you feel you can't make it, for one reason or another, you just let me know. Somebody else can cover it."

Tessa nodded. "I'l let you know what I decide, Beryl—about everything."

Beryl nodded and backed away from the car. "Fair enough. But while you're out there thinking, Tessa, think about this. Things might change, but feelings remain the same. And it's not necessarily what you're committed to that counts. It's to whom."

12

IT WAS WEDNESDAY AFTERNOON. She had four days to decide what to do about finishing the Beryl Mc-Gregor story. But Tessa saw it in more dramatic terms. She felt she had four days to straighten out her entire life.

Not that she didn't have it coming. She had been waiting since when—April?—for this sorting-out process to catch up with her. Putting it off until late June had not, after all, meant that the process would be any easier. It simply meant that she had more to straighten out.

Tessa drove back to Boston and went straight to the station. The first thing she wanted to straighten out was Tim McNulty, who would surely become apoplectic when he found out that Tessa planned no broadcasts on the Beryl McGregor story until the following Monday—and perhaps not even then. Tim would want to know what the hell was going on, and Tessa, even as she walked into his office, had no idea how she was going to explain things. But she knew she would have to do some explaining.

As it turned out she scarcely had to say a word. Just as the receptionist ushered her into the producer's inner office, Tim was hanging up the phone.

He looked up at Tessa and pursed his lips. "I was expecting you," he said. "Come in."

Tessa took a seat. "How could you have been expecting me? I just called you this morning to tell you I was on my way back out to Choate Hollow."

Tim pointed to the phone. "That was Choate Hollow that just hung up. Miss Beryl McGregor, to be exact."

Tessa felt a chasm open up in the pit of her stomach. She was sure Beryl had changed her mind—that she was not going to sit around waiting for Tessa Drew to pull her act together, and that she wanted another reporter out to cover her planned announcement about selling the house. "Well," she muttered, "I guess that's that." In her numbed state, she really didn't find that she cared. All she wanted to do was get farther away.

"That's what?" Tim looked perplexed. "She told me she had sent you back here because she got this one-week extension and she was sick and tired of having you breathing down her neck. She said she wanted some time to think in peace."

Good old Beryl—she had known Tessa would have some tough explaining to do. That lady had a natural knack for the news business. Tessa made a mental note to tell her that when Beryl was ready to decide on her next career.

"Tim, look," Tessa confided. "The truth is, I need a break from this whole thing as much as Beryl does. Can I have this time off? Until Monday, I mean."

Tim looked at her closely, and under his shrewd scrutiny Tessa was forced to lower her eyes. "What's

up with you, anyway?" he asked, coming around to
the front of his desk. "You used to be a pretty hard-
boiled kid when it came to high-emotion pieces like
this one. What's eating at you, Tessa?" He reached
out and lifted her chin up, then pulled his hand away
quickly when he saw the tears suddenly staining
Tessa's cheeks.

"It's not the story, Tim," she whispered. "It's just—
I could really use a few days away from it all, you
know?"

Tim searched the drawn face before him, and
Tessa could see his mind clicking back through all
that had happened since the day he first assigned her
to the story at the request of that environmental
engineer whose name he had forgotten. After a long
pause, during which he apparently reached his own
conclusions, Tim went back around to his side of the
desk and began rummaging through his top drawer.

"A few days off. Yeah, why not?" he muttered,
careful not to meet Tessa's tear-streaked visage. "Listen, as a matter of fact, I've got a great idea." He
tossed a set of keys and a folded piece of paper across
the desk. "Here are the keys to my summer cottage
on the Cape. Directions are in the envelope. Why
don't you scoot down there and really get away?
You've been putting in plenty of overtime lately. I
suppose we can spare you until Miss McGregor's
ready to make up her damned mind. Go on. Take it."

Tessa blinked. "But don't you use the place? I
thought you went down every weekend during the
summer?"

Tim shrugged. "Naaa. I've got to be in town this

weekend anyway. I lend it out a lot. Why do you think I always have the directions handy? I'm not that forgetful."

He was not forgetful at all, and Tessa had an idea that he knew exactly what he was doing by sending her down to the Cape. It was a generous gesture, pure and simple, and she stood up and hugged him for it.

"Thanks, Tim, really. Thanks."

"Thanks, nothing. I expect some superior reporting out of you, old girl, so you'd better make the most of my generosity and pull yourself together, you hear?"

IT WAS THE SECOND ADMONITION she had received that day, not counting her own. First Beryl, now Tim. Everybody seemed to think Tessa needed to sort things out. And Tessa agreed. The question was how to begin. She threw some clothes in a suitcase and drove down to Tim's place on the outer tip of Cape Cod, promising herself that she would get down to business.

The only difficulty was that every time she tried to prioritize her problems—to think about Douglas, for example, or Beryl McGregor—she found herself invariably drawn back to one subject. Thomas Chimatsu.

She could not get beyond the image of him, the feel and smell of him. His name seemed to echo along Route 6, pounding into her consciousness as the wheels pounded the road. T.C., T.C., T.C. . . .

By the time Tessa got to Tim's cottage, she was utterly demoralized by her inability to abolish her longing for T.C. She had always been able to think clearly, she reprimanded herself. This was what she *always* did when she had problems: took herself away somewhere and attacked them as she attacked undesirable news assignments—logically, methodically and exhaustively. Now, all she felt was exhausted.

The cottage was a quiet, restful place and would have been ideal as Tessa's private think tank if she had been able to appreciate its finer points. It was very tiny—a simple, whitewashed rectangle with a screened-in wraparound porch that faced the bay. The stretch of beach in front of it was far less crowded than the public beaches on the ocean side of the Cape, and all the windows faced out on empty sky, land and water. A slatted boardwalk led from her porch right to the edge of the beach, and dune grass grew in spiky fronds up through the spaces in the boards. The air smelled of budding beach plums, citric against the briny tang of the sea.

The first thing she did was get into her swimsuit. It was still quite early in the day, and, as she stood in front of Tim's ancient refrigerator eating a cup of raspberry yogurt, she could feel the chill wrapping around her bare legs, sending goose bumps across her flesh. *Good*, she thought grimly, *maybe the cold air will shock me back to my senses.*

She finished her yogurt, took a deep breath and headed right down to the water's edge. The waves lapped icily at her toes, but she did not step back. There was not a soul in sight at this hour. Good, she thought, no distractions. Except, of course, her own rebellious heart.

Tessa walked for most of that day, veering from her relentless path only when the tide crept up the sand, forcing her to higher ground. She had planned to swim, hoping the cold water would clear her head but the rhythm of her stride was hypnotic, and she could not break from her rigid course. She walked on and on, waiting for some sort of resolution to the refrain that beat a lovelorn cadence against her ear.

But she could not get Thomas Chimatsu out of her mind. She was as filled with the thought of him as her body had been filled with the feel of him. He blocked out any other reality, and for the first time in her life Tessa found herself incapable of rational thought—incapable of any thought, except the presence of him in her body and soul.

IN ALL, she must have passed the sign twenty times that day before she noticed it. It was a small and weathered sign, and it was stuck into the sand at a rakish angle that belied its intimidating message. It was late afternoon before she finally got around to reading the sign.

"Elliott Wildlife Sanctuary," she read. "Private Property. No Fishing, No Hunting, No Picnicking, No Swimming. Police Take Notice."

Tessa stared at it for a full sixty seconds, her lips forming the words over and over again. The Elliott Wildlife Sanctuary, which Thomas Chimatsu had designed and for which he had won the Boston Best award. She sat down hard in the sand, her momentum disrupted at last. "I don't believe this," she muttered, and then burst into loud laughter. The Elliott Sanctuary! Right here, next door to the very spot to which she had come in the hopes of getting away from all that! Life was full of ironies, but this—this had to be the limit!

Tessa lay back in the warm sand, chuckling away and ignoring the heads that turned in her direction. It really was too much. Even since the night she had first met T.C. her life had been full of these ironic coincidences. But now Tessa was prepared to entertain the notion that fate was handing her a not-so-subtle hint. It was one thing to fall in love with a man on the rebound, and to wonder whether that man felt the same about her, but Tessa could no longer ignore the obvious.

Whatever T.C. felt about her—whatever he was able to offer in terms of commitment and fidelity—she must acknowledge that her love and commitment to him was total. Her fears of betrayal, her doubts about her own ability to commit herself had vanished—blown away by the stiff sea breeze that rose off the bay. She loved him. Of course! That was why she had been unable to sort out anything else in her life. There was only one rational conclusion to be reached—she loved T.C., and she must let him know it. No more holding back out of pride or fear.

Now energy surged back through her body so quickly that she felt she might burst. She stood up and waded out until the waves licked around the bottom of her scarlet tank suit. Then she flung herself forward and began to swim. She swam back and forth along the shoreline, along the same path she had followed all day. Every time she lifted her head for a breath she could see it—the soft wall of scrub pine and thick underbrush that marked the edge of the Elliott Sanctuary. It had become a totem for her, and she kept it in sight at all times, smiling each time she lifted her head out of the waves.

By the time she walked out of the water, it was dusk and the beach was empty. Tessa felt drained, but not numbed as she had when she arrived. This was the emptiness of good healthy physical exhaustion, and she knew that she would have no trouble sorting out her options now.

She walked back up to the cottage and grabbed a huge white terry-cloth robe that was hanging on a hook behind the bedroom door. She showered off the salt water and, wrapped in the thick robe, curled up on a wicker rocking chair on the screened-in porch. Night was falling rapidly across the calm water of the bay, and she could hear the blurry call of the night crickets, accompanied by an occasional trill from a lobster buoy out on the water. Despite the fact that she was alone in an isolated spot, she felt no fear. The lights of the nearby town twinkled across the curve of the bay with comforting gaiety, and the narrow porch on which she sat felt familiar and safe as a haven.

Feeling hungry, Tessa got up and took some cheese out of the refrigerator, along with a quart of apple cider and a big bowl of nuts in the shell that she found on the dining-room table. Tucking these under her arm, she went back to the porch, grabbing an old

afghan along the way to ward off the chill of night.
Then she curled back up in the chair to nibble her
meal, swigging cider directly from the jug and waiting patiently for the stars to appear in the velvet sky.

Finally, she was ready to listen to her inner voice,
which had been silent and confused for so long. A
few days earlier—it seemed like years—during their
walk on the river esplanade, T.C. had told her that
she was being too emotional, that she needed to
separate her life from her work and face reality with
the right perspective. All of these accusations were,
in a sense, accurate. But what was amazing was the
fact that, until that moment, no one had ever accused
her of being *overly* emotional. She had always been
the one to stay aloof from emotional entanglements,
the one who always called time out, the one who was
unable to commit herself to anything or anyone. The
one whose perspective separated her forever from the
others. She had been a "typical" Gemini—mercurial
and forever unattached.

She saw now that this had changed. Tessa *had*
been committed—to Beryl, to her job, to Choate
Hollow—almost without knowing why. Because it
had *felt* right—because she had been emotionally involved, against all reason or logic. And she was
proud of it.

As for not being able to deal with her real emotions, Tessa acknowledged that this was probably
true as well. She was so used to *thinking* about how
she should feel that she had almost forgotten how to
just *feel*. That's what came of living too much in the
head and not enough in the heart.

Now, in her new state of emotional clarity, everything seemed to fall into place easily. Beryl would survive and prosper, the Gemini Lakes would become a reality and Tessa's career would continue to develop. But most important, what would happen to her and T.C.? The man had always been, she now realized, a mirror into her true soul. Why had she not seen it before? Why had she run from the image of herself reflected in his eyes? Tessa realized she had not thought about their physical similarities in a long time. She had been too busy magnifying their differences, afraid that, by dwelling on their likeness, she would risk losing herself in him altogether.

But now she thought about it, sitting curled up in the semidarkness with a rueful smile on her face. Their similarities were real—they existed—just as her feelings for him were real. It might take T.C. a while to find out what Tessa already knew, and it might take him even longer to come to grips with it, but Tessa was willing to wait. She loved him, and that was what was most important to her. What was more, she knew that T.C. loved her too. His body could not lie, and now, in the still clarity of night, Tessa recalled that he had tried to let her know how he felt, just as she had tried and failed with him.

Tessa untangled herself from the chair and quilt and got ready to get into bed. They had to talk. She needed to hear from T.C., so that they could talk about what really mattered to them, and perhaps reveal their private fears to each other. But it really didn't matter what he said, or what she said. The point was she was free now to love him.

Wrapped in this assurance, a wistful smile and an old terry robe she fell into a deep and peaceful slumber.

SHE DID NOT KNOW how long she slept when the sound of knocking woke her up. It took Tessa a few seconds to reorient herself in the dark and unfamiliar room and a few more seconds to identify the sound of the voice that was calling her name. But as soon as she did, she flew out of bed and through the cottage to the porch, pulling the door open in one ecstatic sweep.

"T.C.!"

She fell into his open arms, half weeping, half laughing at this final—and more joyous—irony. She had fallen asleep dreaming about driving home to find him, and here he was, having done the same thing for her. Somehow, it made the need for any explanation superfluous.

"You're a dream come true," she said against his ear, and the sound of his triumphant laughter made her realize that her dream really had come true.

"I'm not a dream," he said, half carrying her clinging body inside the cabin. "I've had to do some very real-life detective work to find you, young lady." He sat down in the rocking chair and gathered her onto his lap. "Although I might add, finding you in this delicious state made all my toil worthwhile." He and Tessa both looked down at her half-opened, over-sized robe and laughed.

"How did you?" she asked. "Find me, I mean."

T.C. kissed the bridge of her nose. "I am now in

Tim McNulty's debt," he said. "Although I think he knows that if he hadn't told me, I would have wrung it out of him."

"You went to Tim?"

"After I went to Beryl I went to the station, but he had already gone home for the night. Do you know how many McNultys, Timothy, there are in the Boston phone book?"

Tessa smiled. "You must have wanted to find me very much."

T.C.'s eyes softened. "You'll never know, Tessa, how much."

"Oh, I think I have a pretty good idea."

They stared at each other in rapt silence for a moment. Then T.C. reached down and adjusted Tessa's robe more tightly around her waist. "Come on," he said, "get decent and let's take a little walk. I have some explaining to do, and I can't do it with your body waiting for me like that. By the way, it occurred to me as I drove up here that I'm familiar with this area."

Tessa stood up and held out her hand to him. "The Elliott Sanctuary. I just discovered it this afternoon. It's quite lovely."

"Ironic, isn't it?" T.C. shook his head.

Tessa grinned. "Life," she said, "is full of ironies."

They walked outside into the moonlit night. The beach was deserted, and the water sparkled like jewels on a pale woman's creamy throat. Tessa and T.C. headed toward the sanctuary, holding hands and stepping in unison across the cool sand. Overhead, there was a flutter of raucous trilling, and an answering shriek from within the dense scrub oak that ringed the sanctuary land.

"Hear that? That's a double-crested cormorant," T.C. told Tessa. "If she expects to find nest space over here, she's going to have to fight the tern colony that's lying in wait for her beneath the sea-grape trees."

"How do you know all that from just hearing those calls?"

T.C. smiled. "I'm an ardent environmentalist, remember? Also, it helps that I had to reestablish all this vegetation on land that was badly eroded—and I had to allow for nesting space for all the wildlife— terns, cormorants, black ducks, geese. . . ."He waved his arms at the dense thickets of scrub pine and rose hip bushes that rose up, seemingly right out of the sandy beach. "I like to think of this place as the Ellis Island of aquatic wildlife."

Tessa grinned. "How noble." A sudden scuffle in the thickets at her feet made Tessa start.

"Scared?" T.C. asked, pulling her closer. "We can go back down to the beach, if you'd rather. As a matter of fact, I think I'd rather myself. Somehow, I'm finding small comfort in this sanctuary tonight— even if it is of my own making—or maybe *because* it's of my own making."

They reached the clearing and Tessa looked up at his pale profile. "Why do you say that? It's a beautiful sanctuary, T.C., worthy of a Boston Best, remember?" She leaned over and kissed his cheek.

"I know." He leaned his cheek ruefully against hers for a moment as they walked down the slope of sandy beach to the water's edge. "But lately I've begun to figure out that it's not that important to me—Boston Bests, sanctuaries, even Gemini Lakes...." He stopped and turned to face Tessa, putting both hands on her shoulders so that she had to stop and face him. "What's important is you and I. I want to find out what's happening with you, Tessa Drew. And I want to tell you what's happening with me."

Tessa took a deep breath and leaned slightly into him and away. "Do you want to go first, or shall I?" She was feeling apprehensive, now that the moment of truth was at hand.

T.C. laughed uneasily, and she could sense that he, too, was nervous. It didn't make her feel much better. Was the reality going to be that much less than what she had dreamed it would be? She swallowed hard.

"I'd love to say ladies first and leave it to you, but I can tell you're as nervous as I am." He paused to look at her face, then suddenly pulled her close. "I've never had this happen to me before, Tess. I'm afraid." He kissed the top of her head, then pulled back so he could see her upturned face. "But not so scared that I don't know it's right." He smiled and, tucking her shoulder underneath his, began to walk along the shoreline. "Still, knowing it's right doesn't mean I get off without an explanation, so here goes."

Tessa smiled. It was *right*—he had said so. Her momentary doubts about what was about to happen to them had disappeared completely. It didn't much matter what his explanations were—or hers. All that mattered to her was that he had reached the same conclusion as she had. They were right together.

"First of all," T.C. said, "I want you to know that I never went back on our word—I never tried to get Beryl to change her mind when I went to see her that morning."

Tessa smiled. "I never believed that you did," she fibbed. "Not for a minute."

T.C. hugged her closer. "I went there to talk about us, Tessa. I told Beryl I was afraid our relationship was getting in the way of our careers, that I was afraid my commitment to my work was being jeopardized by my feelings for you. I told her that I wasn't sure it was right for me to be so involved with you—not now, not at this point in my life—and in my career. You know what she told me? She told me I was a jerk, and that if I let the Gemini Lakes get in the way of my love for you then I was being a bigger fool than she had been. That's when she told me she had decided to sell the house. She said she had only been hanging on because she thought she was supposed to, and if people spent their lives doing what they thought they had to, it would be a miserable world to live in."

Tessa smiled. She could hear Beryl saying those words as clearly as if she were speaking them now. But it was T.C. who was speaking, and she gave him her devoted attention.

"On my way to New York," he went on, "I thought about what Beryl had said. And I remembered that morning before I left, when I woke up in your bed beside you." He leaned over and kissed her tenderly, once on each eyelid. "I lay there for a long time watching you while you slept, Tessa."

"I hope I didn't snore." Tessa grinned.

T.C. chuckled. "It wouldn't have mattered if you had. You looked so beautiful, so peaceful . . . so satisfied. I thought to myself, she looks the way I feel when I'm with her! Why should it be so hard to share that with her? Why was I so afraid to express my feelings to you, and why was I so afraid of them myself?"

T.C. paused, and Tessa knew he was coming to the most difficult part. Then he told her about the woman with whom he had shared a four-year relationship—a relationship that had seemed ideal to him, until one day, suddenly, he found himself unable to remain in it any longer. Although their separation had been fairly amicable, T.C. had been saddled with tremendous guilt about it and had vowed never to let his emotions run away with him in such a hurtful way.

"And I thought I was living up to those vows—I thought they made so much sense. But then, lying there beside you, I realized that whatever had happened before in my life—and whatever had happened to you in terms of other relationships—they had nothing at all to do with this one we were experiencing now. I looked at your face and I thought, it looks like my own, but it looks different, too. You were a mirror, a celestial partner in every sense of the word, but you were also a mystery to me. And I discovered that what I wanted to do most in the world was to discover those mysteries with you."

He looked away, and Tessa felt his sense of failure with a deep and sudden pang. "It took me all the way to New York and back before I realized that the only way I could unlock your mysteries was to share mine. I turned around and came straight home without ever going to the conference."

Tessa reached up and placed her fingers gently across his lips. It was her turn, she knew. T.C. must understand that the burden of pride and evasion could be shared. Besides, she had already heard what she wanted to hear.

"All my life," she began without preamble, "I've lived by the rule that emotions should not cloud the intellect. I was a true Gemini, or so I thought—like you, T.C. Until I met you I never had any trouble keeping the two separate, never had any trouble telling people what I felt because it never mattered enough to me one way or the other.

"Then I met you, and your separate-but-equal policy seemed to me to be the pinnacle of intelligent living." She reached up to stroke his cheek. "I thought we were made for each other in that respect. Of course, that was before I began to fall in love with you. Then, everything seemed to get so hard. I was making it so hard for myself, trying to live up to what I *thought* should be."

"We were both making it hard for each other," T.C. said.

Tessa nodded. "You say you had an epiphany of sorts the other night in my bed. Well, I had one too, earlier that night, as we walked along the river. I realized for the first time that, contrary to what I had always believed about myself, I *could* be emotionally committed to a cause, or an issue, or my job." She smiled. "Only I made one little mistake. I thought I was committed to Beryl McGregor and Choate Hollow. I was really committed to you."

T.C. shook his head in a kind of absent wonder. "All this time," he said softly, "the two of us loving each other, and each of us so determined to go on as if nothing had changed in our lives—how could we have been so blind!"

Tessa laughed. "The ever-mutable Twins, hanging on to some ill-guided self-image that kept them from having what they really wanted."

"I was so sure I was right, though!" T.C. was still in the grip of disbelief, and Tessa, for whom the truth had come a lot more easily, watched him struggle to make peace with that part of himself that she knew so well. "I believed in my life!" he exclaimed.

"Don't you still?" She leaned luxuriously into his hands, which were now both framed around her face as if T.C. could find the truth in her features. "I still believe in mine," she said. "It's just that it's changed to include you. Remember, there's nothing wrong with change. The Gemini Lakes should have taught you that."

At last T.C. smiled. "There must be some poetic justice in this, too," he said. "In me having to be told that there's nothing wrong in change." He shook his head and leaned forward to kiss her.

Tessa drank hungrily from his lips and then pulled gently away. "What is this world coming to?" she murmured mockingly.

"I have no idea what it's coming to," T.C. said, slipping both hands in under Tessa's terry-cloth robe.

"And, for the first time in my life, I don't particularly care." His eyes suddenly widened. "Tessa! I thought you got yourself decent before we left the house!"

Tessa tossed her head. "I did."

"But . . . you're stark naked!"

"That," Tessa replied, shrugging the robe off her bare shoulders, "is the general idea."

T.C. paused for only the briefest second before reaching out and grasping her around the waist. He pulled her against him, rubbing his strong thumbs up and down the sensitive striations of her ribs. "Life," he said, as they slipped down onto the sand, "is indeed full of ironies. And wonderful surprises. I'm just learning to take advantage of them."

"Good thing you're a quick study," Tessa said, and then his mouth covered hers, and there was no time for further discussion. They had fallen together on the sand about halfway down the beach, and the tide, which had gone way out, had left cool, damp patches interspersed with the drier, fluffy stuff. The distinction between warm and cool, dry and damp was a shock to Tessa's naked body, but it only enhanced her sensitivity. T.C. slipped off his clothing as easily as she had dropped her robe, and now to the dichotomy of sensation was added a third counterpoint—that of T.C.'s lean frame pressing urgently against hers, all hard and velvety and hot.

Tessa flung her head back into the spun-sugar sand and arched her torso up against him, offering her breasts, her ribs and the narrow slope of her waist to his eager taste and touch. Above her the stars glittered in a dim canopy of light. Tessa smiled heaven-

ward. For someone who didn't believe in fate, she
owed an awful lot to the astrological bodies that spun
out their existence millions of miles away. She still
wasn't sure whether she believed, but right now she
was grateful for the curtain of darkness punctuated
by diamonds above her head—it was a fitting tribute
to her passion and her love for Thomas Chimatsu.

Now his mouth slipped lower, and Tessa could no
longer concentrate on the stars. Her center of consciousness seemed to have moved much closer to the
earth, to the small, burning flame in her hips and
belly that T.C. was inciting to a riotous glow. Eyes
closed, she thrust her fingers into his hair and slipped
her arms beseechingly down along the broad slope of
his shoulders, entreating him to let her share in his
dance of passion.

He twisted around so that they lay face to face on
their sides in the sand. T.C.'s face was soft and misty
with love, and Tessa kissed each feature tenderly. If
Thomas Chimatsu was a mirror into her own soul,
then his body was a temple to her desires, as hers was
to him. Now it was her turn to slip down and caress
him as he had done to her. Tessa had never felt so
open and giving in a relationship before; even when
she had made love with T.C. before she had not felt
this gentle fullness in her heart, this serenity of purpose and intent. There was no fear of discovery on
that deserted beach. Why should there be? The
world, that night, was theirs.

She could feel T.C.'s need vibrating through her.
Her lips over his manhood were gently hungry, seek-
ing to pull him out of himself, to discover that core

she had glimpsed the last time they made love. She wanted to love him until he could bear it no longer, just as he had done for her.

But then T.C.'s strong arms reached down and pulled her up alongside him again. "What you are doing is driving me crazy," he breathed, covering her mouth with his own.

"I want that," she murmured back between breathless kisses. "I want you to lose yourself in me as I have lost myself in you."

T.C.'s fingers slipped across her throat and down to her breasts. He pressed them gently into her flesh, creating whorls of flames from the tips outward to the sensitive skin beneath her arms. His strong thighs and urgent maleness pressed against her loins creating the same pattern of desire, an elegant tattoo against her burning flesh.

But he pulled his face away and shook his head. "Not this time. This time we lose our hearts to each other together. Because this time," he added with a hungry kiss, "this time is forever."

Then he slipped his arms around her back to pillow it and, gently parting her thighs, eased himself inside her with exquisite patience. Tessa's eyes slipped shut and she sighed and shuddered in the same breath—a breath that was cut off with a gasp as T.C. dropped his mouth heavily over hers. It was a kiss of endless passion—an endless kiss that was to last all through the final throes of their embrace, as if the ultimate gift from one body to another was that fiery point of contact. And all the while T.C. was deep within her, and Tessa felt his surging power fill her with a wild joy that came near to pain. She felt as if she might be losing consciousness, and she clung to those lips for dear life.

Finally, Tessa felt herself melting into the sand, and T.C. melting into her. The beach became a molten sea of heat and light, and the stars, which had twinkled so many light-years away, dipped down to touch their bodies with an astral flame. They were bonded now, twins forever, by the commitment of their bodies as well as their hearts.

It took a long time for the starry chaos to recede and for the world to right itself into the proper division of earth and sky. Tessa was surprised to find that T.C.'s mouth still covered hers, just as his body was a blanket above her. Slowly, and with that infinite patience she had come to expect from him, he guided their bodies back into separate planes of space, and finally, as if it were the most unbearable separation of all, his lips lifted from hers.

"I think this means you're mine forever," he murmured against her ear, and Tessa was surprised to feel the moist heat of tears against her cheek. She raised her hand to wipe them away. "Are these mine or are they yours?" she whispered.

T.C. lifted his face and she saw that his eyes were wet. Then he bent down and kissed hers, and licked his lips. "Both, I think," he murmured. "And anyway, it doesn't seem to matter. What's mine is yours."

"And what's mine is yours." They smiled at each other over the solemnity of this vow. Tessa arched her neck to look at the beach around her, and at the line of trees that marked the entrance to the Elliott Sanctuary. "I suppose that means all this is mine," she mused, "since you created it."

He shrugged and kissed the spot between her breasts. "I think Charles Daniel Elliott might have a thing or two to say about that—if he were here to say it, which he is definitely not, thank goodness."

Tessa closed her eyes, luxuriating in his touch. "It's a lovely sanctuary," she said.

"Never consecrated until this moment."

"And the Gemini Lakes are going to be beautiful, too," Tessa added. "I really believe that, T.C."

"You should," he joked, but Tessa knew he was pleased with her statement of confidence in him. "It's strange," he added, "how our life together seems to be so bound up in water—I thought we're supposed to be an air sign."

"Haven't you learned the most important thing about a Gemini?" she asked him. "The only thing that remains the same about a Gemini is constant change."

"Not true. Now there is another constant in my life—you."

Tessa smiled and linked her arms around his neck. "The nicest thing about being a twin," she said, pulling him against her once more, "is that there's so little need to talk."

Take these 4 best-selling novels FREE

ANNE MATHER — born out of love

VIOLET WINSPEAR — time of the temptress

CHARLOTTE LAMB — man's world

SALLY WENTWORTH — say hello to yesterday

Harlequin Presents...

Take these
4 best-selling novels
FREE

Yes! Four sophisticated,
contemporary love stories
by four world-famous
authors of romance
FREE, as your
introduction to the Harlequin Presents
subscription plan. Thrill to **Anne Mather**'s
passionate story BORN OUT OF LOVE, set
in the Caribbean.... Travel to darkest Africa
in **Violet Winspear**'s TIME OF THE TEMPTRESS....Let
Charlotte Lamb take you to the fascinating world of London's
Fleet Street in MAN'S WORLD.... Discover beautiful Greece in
Sally Wentworth's moving romance SAY HELLO TO YESTERDAY

Join the millions of avid Harlequin readers all over the
world who delight in the magic of a really exciting novel.
EIGHT great NEW titles published EACH MONTH!
Each month you will get to know exciting, interesting,
true-to-life people .... You'll be swept to distant lands you've
dreamed of visiting .... Intrigue, adventure, romance, and
the destiny of many lives will thrill you through each
Harlequin Presents novel.

Harlequin Presents...

The very finest in romance fiction

Get all the latest books before they're sold out!

As a Harlequin subscriber you actually receive your personal copies of the latest Presents novels immediately after they come off the press, so you're sure of getting all 8 each month.

Cancel your subscription whenever you wish!

You don't have to buy any minimum number of books. Whenever you decide to stop your subscription just let us know and we'll cancel all further shipments.

Your FREE gift includes

Anne Mather—Born out of Love
Violet Winspear—Time of the Temptress
Charlotte Lamb—Man's World
Sally Wentworth—Say Hello to Yesterday